THE DICHOTIC DILEMMA

The Fabric of Life

RT CHIWUTA

The Dichotic Dilemma
The Fabric of Life

Copyright © 2023 by RT CHIWUTA

Paperback ISBN: 978-1-63812-812-0
Ebook ISBN: 978-1-63812-813-7

All rights reserved. No part in this book may be produced and transmitted in any form or by any means, electronic, or mechanical, including photocopying, recording, or by any information storage and retrieval system, without permission in writing from the copyright owner.

The views expressed in this work are solely those of the author and do not necessarily reflect the views of the publisher hereby disclaims any responsibility for them.

Published by Pen Culture Solutions 08/09/2023

Pen Culture Solutions
1-888-727-7204 (USA)
1-800-950-458 (Australia)
support@penculturesolutions.com

THE DICHOTIC DILEMMA

This book is dedicated to my family, near and far.

PROLOGUE

The culmination of this book is a process and a result, at present, of 26 years of human existence. 21 of which were characterised by extreme angst, emotional disillusionment, and difficulty coming to terms with the state of human existence along with my own existence. The early years were a constant battle with mainly the issues of race as that was the first primary realisation. A deep emotional connection with the perceived effects of racism but also a deep emotional connection with the wider aspects of human suffering. Growing up in Zimbabwe in Southern Africa, particularly with South Africa a close neighbour, the function of racial segregation was vividly apparent. This was further emphasised by a historical perspective into the observation of recent history where black people were marginalised and generally second-class citizens. Race and human suffering was all I saw.

All things can reach a crescendo, and the peak of my angst resulted in an intrinsic need to expel my frustrations, thoughts, and feelings for they raked my consciousness near enough every waking minute. Writing became the medium. "What is the purpose of life?" was the cry. Hence, a spontaneous process of catharsis occurred and I began to write down and purge all my thoughts and feelings. A process which filled many notebooks with expressions which were at times poetic, a stream of consciousness and mostly just an expression of political, social, and philosophical ideas. Consequently, the next natural instinct was to transfer these ideas into another medium which then resulted in the writing of this book.

At 21 years of age, yes I had written a book, however, it was the strangest sensation whereby, after completing the book and getting it published, I almost immediately became disillusioned with everything I had written. The clarity I had acquired from cleansing my mind of my thoughts, allowed me to then see a brand new world I had never seen before.

Hence, engraved in me became a strong sense of a lack of confidence in what I had written, consequently, a lack of confidence in myself. In the process of writing the book, I had felt inspired, but once it had been written, and with a blank slate again if you wish, I felt as though I knew nothing.

As ever, life continued. One needs money in this life, so I completed my university education and started a career in the health service. I lost a love that at one stage had seemed so vivid and powerful and experienced all the heartbreak and pain that such a thing can cause. However, many other things stayed the same, and some other things have begun. Through it all however, I got a chance to learn the necessity of pain. In time again, the lessons I have learnt, my experiences, observations, and perceptions of life have led me to sit down and write in an effort to address my disillusionment and hopefully provide a positive perspective on human existence.

Reaching this stage has been aided by the fact that I have been living in England now for over a decade and on that basis, I have been living in the West for more than a decade. I have seen life now from a different perspective, a Western perspective. I have walked, talked, and laughed now amongst people that seemed so separate and alien to me in my younger days. I am now aware of their humanity as I was aware of the humanity of the Africans I had grown up amongst, humanity in its variant forms and manifestations. The world and life now has a new meaning. Therefore, it is on this basis that I now understand my sense of disillusionment when I initially wrote the book earlier on in my life. I would argue that it was a subconscious realisation that perhaps the ideas I had proposed were underdeveloped, preliminary and potentially poorly structured. Hence, now I have the confidence to readdress these issues in a more structured way with a better understanding of the ideas I had accidentally came across as I was initially writing the book.

For five years now, I have not revisited the book to truly know its contents as I did not read it once I had written it. All I know now is that I have a sense of needing to bring order to an unfinished work and in many ways feel grateful to have the opportunity to do so for whatever it might be worth. So, it shall again be a voyage of discovery as I look to connect with the young man I was then and try and amalgamate his ideas with a new found perspective.

The format of the book sees me write down the poems, expressions or ideas that I expelled into my notebooks then following that I try to provide an extrapolation into the hidden meaning of each of the poems or expressions. In the process, I try to discuss ideas and create a platform for understanding my angst and also provide a perspective into human existence..

I will now outline my position.

Initially I will declare my position by saying, above all, I am a human being, which I believe to be the utmost realisation one can make. Not a black man, or an African, or any other description, but a human being. It is a universal concept that breaches and transcends all subdivisions by which we can stand against each other. On that basis, a human being and humanity becomes something much greater than its individual parts, presentations, and subdivisions.

I believe that the basis for understanding is observation, observation and logical balanced deduction. On that basis, I proclaim my position as I look to discuss the phenomenon of human existence as simply one of an observer, an outsider looking in. I propose to offer a neutral exposé based on my understanding of the concept of the Dichotic Dilemma, the input of the basic survival instinct to our every actions, and our perspective and presentation of life powered by our relatively higherfunctioning minds as human beings on this planet, with every observable phenomenon based on a spectrum extending from one extreme to another, positive to negative. The vehicle for this argument is a reductionist assessment of the writings I wrote in my notepads, the poems, thoughts and feelings as I look for meaning and understanding of the human emotional state of being. So in essence, the book becomes an observation of the interplay between the emotional state, and the logical balanced state of being. Ignorance versus understanding, knowledge versus a lack of it, positive versus negative. Essentially, it's the Dichotic Dilemma, and how it affects our day to day existence from intra, inter, micro to macro interaction with ourselves as human beings, the wider world and the Universe at large.

What is the Dichotic Dilemma??

The Dichotic Dilemma is a personal perspective and realisation of a concept that has always existed through the ages. The concept of Balance. Balance is the integral universal phenomenon and the Dichotic Dilemma becomes a personal realisation of how transcendent this concept of balance is with particular reference to the realm of human existence. Hence why I titled the book, The Dichotic Dilemma, the fabric of life. The aim is to try and express this concept throughout the book as we try and extrapolate meaning from the poems.

Suffice it to say, this brings me to quite a subject at this early stage, the subject of God.

As beings on this planet, we are only aware of our existence. Throughout the ages, we have been alive and always grappling with the idea of the purpose of our existence in light of the turmoil of our existence, at times, through our own hand and the hand of powers beyond our measure. God, or Gods in some instances, either become a figure of worship so we can be kept safe, or a figure of derision as we are apparently left to the most ill fates, or God is not considered at all. This then presents a myriad of dilemmas which manifest in many ways as we go through the ages and pursue the objectives of our survival in the context of social existence.

Thus, I propose my perception of the idea of God, a perception which encapsulates the concept of *Balance* and its transcendent nature throughout our existence as human beings. This includes both the positive and negative aspects and includes our place in a magnificent Universe which exceeds our comprehension and are a part of yet seem so separate from. I propose that God is the Universe. I certainly hope that I do not lose vast sways of the readership as I make this proposal. In my view, the concept does not seem that foreign as I ponder these ideas on a daily basis. However, to a world full of such disparate perspectives, the mere suggestion might seem wholly ridiculous. On this basis, I hasten to say, a furthered understanding, I believe, is based on assessing a different or alternate perspective and allowing it to bolster, corroborate, shift, change or maintain your current position based on an objective analysis of that perspective.

Yes, I propose that God is the Universe, which makes us then a part of that Universe and a part of God; in other words, God's children as proposed by some faiths. On that basis, everything else then becomes a part of God, meaning the animals and all other manner of being. Hence, we owe them respect and reverence as we respect ourselves. I am opposed to the more "humanised" idea of God who is a man who speaks of anger, vengeance, and other aspects of human emotion because God should be perfect and complete, thus is beyond the whims of human emotion. On that basis, the only thing imaginable that can resemble perfection, wholeness, and completion is the Universe.

The Universe contains everything and is the perfect balance of opposing forces. It is eternal. Hence, understanding the concept of balance is understanding God. Therefore, we have been set a challenge to attempt to achieve this through human existence.

Some teachings claim that we are created in God's image. On that basis, let us delve into the world of science. Science, in my view, is just the process of objective deduction with a view to understand and manipulate. We at times fear it because it gives the human being great power. Yes for positive outcomes but indeed, at times, negative outcomes depending on your point of observation. Yes, the Dichotic Dilemma. However, the observations and discoveries made through science have informed us now that on the microscopic level, our bodies are made up of fundamental particles; atoms, which contain a nucleus or centre, which is made up of protons and neutrons. These atoms are surrounded by rings of electrons which circle around that centre and this becomes the source of life, the source of structure. Again, science lets us know that the celestial bodies in the Universe which exist beyond our earthly plane resemble the same patterns and structures in variant forms. In addition, everything else that is, shares the same basic structure and elements showing our truly intrinsic interconnectedness with the Universe. If we are not more like God or more like the Universe in our design, then nothing else is.

Indeed, my writing has already taken a dramatic tangent into the realm of the hypothetical at this early stage. Hence, I will bring the reader back to terra firma and discuss the further pillars forming the basis of my discussion. We will revisit the topic of God at later stages in the book.

The survival instinct is the fundamental human input, the fundamental human reflex, the fundamental input and reflex of any animate creature. It is this fact, coupled with our higher-functioning minds in relation to other presentations of life on this planet that creates the human social realm of existence. As human beings, we are able to think and feel in a complex way and our intelligence allows us to exist beyond just the range of instinct, but to be emotionally and intellectually complex. Our minds allow us to ponder and create such things as right and wrong, justice, politics, technology, good and bad, religion, art and abstract ideas and thought processes. As opposed to just instinctive perceptions of fear, fight and flight that are more existent in the lesser minded creatures and beings on the planet. We are not distinct or separate from the laws of nature, we just perceive them in more abstract ways due to our intelligence as opposed to just fundamentally through instinct and some emotional cues.

Life presents itself through the input of individuals in an earth-based social sphere through time and we interact powered by our idiosyncrasies and similarities as individuals and groups, creating an existence, our existence, in this plane. This is all encompassed within a spectrum of extremes from positive to negative with regards to the inputs of every existential variable which contributes to our lives as human beings. It highlights the importance of understanding the concept of balance as a fundamental teaching which will then contribute to a more harmonious existence amongst human beings.

The only then remaining question is, why? Hopefully we can expand on this age-old question as we delve into the book.

Therefore, my attempt in this book and with this book is to try and apply a functional perspective to more abstract ideas using the pillars for debate that I have discussed and identified above. This will allow me to try and deliver some insight into human action and existence beyond the idea that others are good and others are bad or evil. I find the idea to be too simplistic as it negates the input of, I believe, more intrinsic variables and factors which can shed some light into who and what we are and why we act in the ways we do as individuals and groups.

So join me, please, as we delve into my emotional response to life and my perceptions as I attempt to understand them. This is because, I believe that understanding our emotions, actions and perceptions is the way to understanding ourselves, who and what we are and maybe, why we are. We shall go back five years to the beginning of this odyssey of self-expression and begin the journey from there.

Please read on.

INTRODUCTION!!

My name is Raleigh Thandazani Chiwuta, which, before I even begin, is a paradox in itself. My forename is an English man's name which is curious because I am of African descent. My second name is Ndebele, which is a tribe found in Zimbabwe. My surname is Chiwuta which is Shona, another tribe found in Zimbabwe. Therefore, in that alone are a lot of contradictions or amalgamations showing that a lot has transpired through the transition of time and a lot of things have been "moved out of their place of origin". I am 21 years old at present as I write, 21 years, 5 months, and 28 days old to be exact. If I have done this correctly, it should tally with the fact that I was born on the 23rd of November in 1984 as a Zimbabwean.

On the day that I emerged from my mother's nourishing womb, I could never have begun to fathom the complexities of the life I was being delivered into.

I do not remember much of my childhood as is usually the case, from about birth to four years of age. However, as far as I can remember, I have always been very analytical and questioning as a person and very aware of the dynamics of life prevailing around me and trying to make sense of them to figure out what it all means. This is what I believe has led me to sit down and write in an effort to see if I can express my perceptions to the world.

I find the world to be a very complex place. A place where there are exponentially more questions than answers. For example, why is the world the way it is? Why do we do the things we do? Why are we alive? What are we? Why do human beings suffer at times, and what is the purpose of emotional turmoil and pain? And above all, what is the purpose of an existence that pits us against each other, groups and individuals from the day we are born? The resultant consequence is the need to survive and express dominance that, at times, leads us to great acts of murderous violence and malevolence against each other.

With this in mind, the frustration of what happened around me was truly beginning to get the better of me and I was becoming increasingly more frustrated. Frustrated with my never-ending search for answers and coming to constant dead ends and blanks. I was under great emotional and psychological pressure trying to balance out the complex conundrums of human existence. I was drowning in ideas of fairness, famine, injustice, war, death, political unrest, and all other manner of negative consequence that can befall human beings during our existence. I had a very negative perception of life. Things that used to make me happy were now only having a momentary effect. However, I was fortunate in that I had an amazing and good support system, in the form of a loving family, and excellent parents who showed sacrifice, patience, and provided good guidance.

I found solace and respite in the proverbial pen and paper and what emerged were my inner thoughts and feelings, ventilation, my never-ending affair with societal dynamics, and the constant, insistent and incessant ramblings in my mind. My father told me it was poetry. Yes, some of it is poetry, the voice of my subconscious, a marvellous cathartic experience, without which I am not sure of what end I would have reached.

However, I should say that what I found, I had to say, was wide-ranging and referenced many aspects of life. Thus, many ideas will be expressed in this book. Hopefully, the message is coherent and useful as my aim is to try and offer a positive and constructive outlook on life which highlights the pragmatic challenges of existence which always require us to appeal to our better nature.

Chapter One!!

The Underst Ing Of The Concept Of Balance Is The Ultimate Understanding.

1.1 "Civilisation is the ability to curb your basic instinct."

This is the most important and fundamental assertion I will make in this book. It is apt that it is the first point made. In many ways, I feel this is the root source of what we term "human suffering." Our minds allow us to create and perceive politics, notions of right and wrong, good and bad religion and such abstract ideas and thought patterns. Hence, actions based on the survival instinct are then processed and interpreted as either right or wrong by human beings depending on how they affect the individuals involved. Emotions then become the vehicle through which the experience of these inputs colour the perception of our existence. As human beings, the emotional state is what adds feeling to our existence and that is why we experience emotional hurt and pain along with joy and elation depending on the attributes of the prevailing experience.

When civilisations collided through the passage of time, western civilisations had the upper hand technologically. On this basis, they conquered other groups and termed some as civilised or not based on how they lived their lives. However, my perception of civilisation is that it is a function of how we act with regards to how we treat each other and how we treat the planet. Killing and fighting are basic intellectual functions which are powered by the need to survive. To be civilised in the way which is idealised, human beings will have to operate in a way that demonstrates higher mental function in that the lesser basic urges are curtailed in the name of peace and understanding. When we continue to fight and oppress each other, no matter how technologically advanced we become, we will not be civilised, because it will be evidence of being subject to our basic instincts. Hence the notion expressed that civilisation is the ability to curb your basic instinct.

As long as dictatorships, unfair and unrepresentative political and economic systems which benefit others and mean that inevitable social stratification leaves others in dire poverty whilst others opulent beyond imagine continue to exist, we are truly not civilised. But just a higher cognitive-functioning earthly, being subject to the dictates of basic urges.

1.2 "The ultimate knowledge is the knowledge of self."

As a second assertion to be made, this point correlates with and corroborates very well the first fundamental assertion with regards to the relationship between civilisation and the basic instinct.

Understanding yourself and getting to know who you are is important for realising clarity of purpose and can bring balance to one's existence. A mind that is in a state of confusion is an unstable mind, a volatile mind which can then lead to an unstable, volatile, and coarse emotional state. That instability can then be brought to bear to the detriment of the individual and others through adverse unbalanced actions.

Hence, understanding self becomes an avenue towards bringing balance and addressing the extremes of the Dichotic Dilemma to the benefit of the individual and the wider world. The Dichotic Dilemma dictates that, naturally, existence is based on there being extremes and how they interplay to create balance and order. As human beings, understanding this concept, our basic survival instincts with regards to the fundamentals of who and what we are as an existent species in a way that's cohesive, is important to bring balance and order to our existence.

Existent amongst human beings are disparate groups and individuals, some at polar opposites and some similar, yet all should and do have a place on this planet. In the realm of science, through history, curious minds have sought to understand the fundamental aspects of the world around us. That knowledge gained is the vehicle behind twenty-first-century technology where it is applied, and has relieved the yoke of some of the more limiting aspects of human existence. Yet, the benefits

of this knowledge are not equally distributed within micro and macro society and societies at large. Hence, the necessity for us as a species to understand what our fundamental motivations are and adjust them to always accommodate the needs of others around us. Then by realising our similarities, build back up from that knowledge a way of existing that limits the yoke of the consequences of the more limited aspects of our nature.

Consequently, understanding ourselves, our basic nature and how it affects our more abstract existence is a route to which we can create a better life for ourselves. Hence why, the knowledge of self is the ultimate knowledge. Understanding our lesser nature is the vehicle to bettering our greater nature. It creates balance and addresses the Dichotic Dilemma wherein everything is influenced by the contribution of opposing forces and a balanced outcome is always the greatest state of existence.

1.3 "Ignorance is the gift of malevolence for it blinds you such that you cannot even see the shackles that bind your hands and feet. It restricts your movement such that you only move in the direction that those who wish to oppress you want you to and you are happy. Blissful oblivion, there is no bliss in such a wretched Curse."

I grew up in Africa and in my youth I was heavily politicised by virtue of the presentation of the world I was seeing which frustrated me greatly, due to the economic and social imbalance and division primarily along racial lines which occluded my perception of other variables.

Zimbabwe, like many former English colonies, is a Christian country, so the influence of biblical thinking and tone will be evident in the expressions I am attempting to understand. Yet now, I think and observe from a different perspective. Consequently, some of the poems will have strong racial and religious overtones which surprise even me as I read back on them and type, looking to offer clarity to an emotionally heightened state of perception. In many ways, the lesson is the reiteration of the point that perspective creates opinion and understanding contrasting perspectives breeds understanding between seemingly disparate points of view.

That clarified, from this poem, I will just focus on the point it raises in regards to ignorance. As I have mentioned, perception and opinion is a function of perspective. Thus, ignorance becomes a function of erroneous perspective and perception and the ramifications of ignorance can cause dire consequences in the human social sphere.

Consequently, understanding extremes and extremes of perceived ignorance is the vehicle to understanding disparity, the Dichotic Dilemma, and creating balance within the human social sphere.

The next poem is about love, and as I rewrite this book, I am having dilemmas about how to restructure it. The feedback I have received about this book is, if anything, to try and structure it by having similarly themed poems together to give the book more cohesion and transferability. However, I believe in fluidity of expression, stream of consciousness as a better format for observing the subconscious. As this book is an analysis of the subconscious, and how it can and does motivate human behaviour and thoughts, I am becoming more emboldened in maintaining this format of random thoughts as I feel it reflects the human being and experience more poignantly. The human existential experience is not divided into separate entities. We experience and perceive all aspects of existence as they present and in their amalgamation on a day-to-day basis all at once. Politics, love, religion, war and everything else all at once and perceive them as they shape us individually per experience into whom and what we are.

Hence, why I believe in expatiating on each notion, idea, or poem in the order in which it entered my consciousness. I hope the reader can appreciate this notion and find enjoyment from reading the book presented in this format.

To understand the human being and experience is to understand it as it presents. Life does not occur in what we would deem an ordered way; that is why we struggle with it. Bringing sense and understanding to an apparently disordered presentation I suggest, is a way to understand it and bring balance to it. I certainly hope to draw on sustainable conclusions with regards to this point by the end of this book. So, moving on........

1.4 "Love is the "pure" sacrifice of oneself for another. It is best described as an act because it can only be shown. When you love, you cannot help but love and you cannot help but show it. It is the most powerful emotion and with great power comes great responsibility hence great risk and danger. It has the power to build and the power to destroy, hence great care is needed thus it can only be shown. It is circular because to love, you have to be able to show affection and it is only in this ability that the real strength of love lies in its expression. The power of love lies in its expression, in its overt expression."

Love is a very complex emotion and human emotions are a complex phenomenon. When I wrote this, I was young and still learning about love. Oftentimes, love is depicted as something where everything is perfect and in many ways, in my youth that could have been my view of it when innocence was untainted. However, in an "imperfect" world, a world where there are positive and negative aspects to existence, creating our perceived ideas of perfection is difficult if not impossible.

Some have tried. An easily transferable example is Hitler and the Nazis for the love of their land and people. This is where love becomes, indeed, a complex subject. It poses great social dilemmas and contradictions as the notion of it is attempted to be expressed by humanity in a volatile world full of disparities and disparate peoples.

On that basis, an analysis of what love is reveals that it is an extreme feeling. The antithesis of hate in purist terms. Yet out of love and for love, hurt and hate for others can occur. The manifestation of the Dichotic Dilemma. As expressed before, this is a phenomenon that transcends all aspects of human existence and existence universally. Everything can have either a positive or negative effect depending on how it is expressed and managed. Love equally so. As mentioned before, it is an extreme feeling, so in essence, it is a phenomenon to an extreme, meaning it can produce extreme results. That is why we can die for love, and equally so, kill for love. As the poem purports, true love is its expression, but I would argue, positive expression to all. For example, what becomes of the people who love their country so much and do not want foreigners in it? Therein lies the effect of the Dichotic Dilemma as it pervades and manifests itself in the sphere of human social existence. Look deep enough, then you realise that the so-called love for their country is based on survival.

By virtue of our existence and differences, the Dichotic Dilemma, survival instinct and our higher-functioning minds, these variables pit us against each other, to war and hate at times, all in the name of love. My purpose is to try and express these ideas to highlight a possible perspective behind why we act the way we do. That is why at the beginning of the book, I denounced the concept of good and evil because it is shallow. The reason being, based on the example of the nationalists not wanting foreigners in their country, a so-called foreigner needing access to that country and not being allowed could deem those people bad or evil. Yet those nationalists love their daughters and sons and live normal lives but are just protecting what is theirs for the sake of their survival and that of their children.

Hence, instead of good or evil, a better position is to argue in terms of perspective and perception. No human being is born "evil", so to speak. To see a newly born infant is to observe what humanity truly is in its basic state. It writhes and wriggles and only looks for the tit to breastfeed. It is a primal observation that sheds light to the origins of our nature when we are older. No one can say that babies are evil, yet they grow into one spectrum, rapists and murderous, and to the other spectrum, altruistic philanthropists and many other things in between. No one can say they are wholly good or wholly bad all their life. Yet some indeed do exist on one side of the spectrum more than the other in terms of their consequence to others. So, how can we define good and evil? It is said that, the scientists who designed the nuclear bomb and saw its result, many of them so shocked at what they had done, decided to turn to biology to pour their efforts into something to help mankind. Can we say they were evil?

Or were they products of a human existential perspective which shaped their behaviour according to their attributes and designed a weapon of death looking after the needs of their survival, who, in the process, unleashed tremendous disaster? This is the power of the Dichotic Dilemma when forces are pushed to extremes. Their survival against the survival of others. Both sides in this battle would have argued their position as the good ones.

Life's dilemmas are plenty and go beyond the shallow perceptions of good and evil because those alienate a disparate but singular human race by creating the most extreme state of them and us. We say we are civilised and the fore being on this planet. Surely we can express that claim to a better consequence than we do. Or are we just designed to be the way we are and incapable of anything else and bound to repeat history! Indeed the Dichotic Dilemma!

1.5 "We live in the times of revelations. "MONEY", the evidence is all around us, The Devil is alive and at work. Ignorance is his main ally, hence the unforeseen carnage that prevails today. For he has made it so that everything can distract the mind so we can never know the truth."

As I mentioned before, by virtue of my religious upbringing, my definition of the things I observed in my youth was coloured by religious overtones. Yet again, it becomes a matter of perspective.

As mentioned at the beginning of the book, I do not believe in the personified idea of God. Consequently, the same belief pertains to the Devil. Certainly, in religious teachings, especially in Christianity as I am more familiar with it, the Devil is someone or something that influences us to do bad things. I remember being young and at church being told to listen and you can hear the good and the bad angel influencing you on how to act in a situation. This is what we call the conscience.

Certainly, that is without denial. I am sure everyone experiences that discourse in their mind as we go about making our decisions with some more inclined to being at each end of the spectrum. However, again, as has been proposed, to speak of evil is to not look deep enough. The real question to ask is why we experience this in the first place. Evil suggests absolute free choice and absolute free will. However, I suggest that free will is a very relative and limited function predicated upon by the pillars I have mentioned: instinct, the Dichotic Dilemma, and our higher-functioning minds which are influenced and present in myriad ways by virtue of circumstance. The question then again to ask, is, if not free will, the devil and evil, then who and what are we, and why are we here?

Again, the mention of money as a spectre of evil is the result of, I believe, religious indoctrination which has a powerful effect on perceptions and perspective. It is a variable in many ways that should be used with the deepest wisdom and care. Another dilemma indeed. In any case, with regards to money, fundamentally, it is a route towards survival.

Chasing it and overvaluing its importance above all else is abiding to the dictates of the basic survival instinct with the resultant effects being the perceived carnage mentioned in the poem.

1.6 "I have loved.
For me, love is you and you are love.
The good and the bad, I just hope we can work
it out for she has conquered my heart in a
way it can never be conquered again.
She is the personification of beauty and all
things beautiful about this world.
She is raw, she is beautiful, and I love her.
Hopefully we can unite forever."

Some say, if you have ever truly loved someone, no matter what, you will always love them, and indeed love them till your last day. It is certainly good and edifying to hold on to our more positive attributes. Love is one of them, and when love is applied in a way that truly conquers our lesser selves, the true value of the phenomenon can be realised individually and collectively. I am still a young man at twenty six years of age, but I would say, I have already learnt greatly from experiencing and coming through the torments which can arise from deep emotional commitment. Definitely, a brighter side to life can be realised from this. It is a unifying notion, a notion based on understanding.

1.7 "Black is Supreme, Black is paramount, Black is imperious,
Black is powerful, Black is impregnable, Black is eternal,
Black is me and I am black, a black man.
Black cannot be unleashed for it holds a power so
great that if unleashed it will resonate and
reverberate through the galaxy.

Black is ancient, Black is everlasting,
Black is true and the truth will liberate
even the weariest of souls.
Black is true and I am black. Black is amazing,
Black is complex, Black is simple, Black, oh my God,
Black is the sleeping giant, the sleeping elephant
that cannot wake up for if it does,
"TREMBLE".
Oh you better "TREMBLE" ye who
drugs, rapes, belittles and tortures me.
"TREMBLE".

This is one of my more inflamed and racially charged pieces. I am a black man, and in this period of existence, it certainly has its challenges. Africa, the stronghold of black civilisation is a continent crippled by, in many ways, malfunctioning postcolonial political systems that oppress their own people. Burdened by relative economic strife and an infrastructural vacuum, Africa is a continent home to a group of people who could be forever struggling to catch up with a rapidly technologically progressing world. The black race, for a large part in recent history, has had its name and reputation systematically tarnished through a recent era of economic, psychological and physical subjugation.

Through industrialised slavery, and systematic oppression, the black race has, in many ways, been the blood sweat and tears behind the infrastructural and technological advancement of the western world in recent history. However, through civil pressure and a change in industrial mechanics, the period of industrialised large scale slavery in recent history passed. Coupled with an end of overt military and physical colonial imperialism for the greater part of the latter century. However, the by-product of this has been the disenfranchisement of the black race with "ghettoisation" and relegation to second class citizenship-hood throughout many parts of the globe.

This is also characterised through this period by years of systematic torture and social stigmatisation and labelling that has left the black race with a less than honourable reputation by many accounts. This is what I am writing against and emboldening my consciousness against through this piece of writing. To be told you are something that every part of you tells you that you are not; thieves, beggars, the lowest strata of existence. Yet it seemed to be evidenced in the presentation of the social stratification I was observing growing up. Nonetheless, that notion I just could not see in my family and in the people around me. All I saw were human beings. Indeed for a time, that observation was colour coded in response to the colour coding thrust onto me.

Although colour coding is not the ultimate factor, it is certainly a factor still, as it is naive to discount the ramifications that difference causes. Hence why the ultimate realisation is the realisation of human strife throughout the continuum of time. Not individual strife but to realise the functional inputs which contribute to human existence, the more intrinsic human story. The one that dictates that suffering is not just the bedfellow of the black race, that joy has also been a part of that suffering. The perception of suffering can be individual and collective, inter- and intra-personal, inter- and intra-racial, inter- and intra- societal. This is the input of the structures that govern human existence, Power and Politics and the fallout from how these processes are conducted and manifest themselves in different geographical locations through time on the planet. The more intrinsic story about what makes us human - a collective group. That is the story I want to tell. That is the realisation that unifies seemingly disparate entities. To realise that our life and existence is but a series of emotional highs and lows based on the perceptions of each individual. Based on the personal experience played out individually in a cosmic plane beyond us but here on earth powered by our differences and similarities, urges, and interactions which can bring us to arms at times as we seek to necessitate our survival. This process transcends all boundaries, races and divisions. Observing humanity as a whole is the crucial first step to understanding a greater purpose and how it could manifest itself.

Understanding the necessity of balance with regards to our existential dilemmas is another important step. Indeed, there is relativity to human existence, but all the fundamental factors are the same.

1.8 "Knowledge is power, knowledge is the truth.
Right knowledge is power and the truth.
Knowledge gives you the power to have your own mind,
and having your own mind will liberate you from the
grasp of those who can influence you negatively.
For everyone on earth is a person, and a
person is just that, a person. Liable to all the traps set for us.
So the ultimate knowledge is the knowledge that lets you
know your own mind and gives you autonomy of self.
Autonomy of purpose.
And this knowledge should always be the truth".

This poem is about knowledge and the truth and I perceive the truth as being the function of balanced, open, and objective observation and deduction.

The information contained in the mind is the vehicle behind action. In a world where people can kill each other based on perspective, to create peaceable co-existence, having the right knowledge is important.

Hence, I argue that the right knowledge should be the truth. Lying is the lowest form of communication because it inhibits understanding and prevents the mind from attaining the appropriate perspective. Lying is appealing to our lesser nature, to the basic survival instinct because its function is to either evade or ensnare. Consequently, to function at a higher level of perception, the mind has to be informed of the truth, especially the perceived harsher aspects of the truth. It is through understanding and dealing with the most difficult and limiting aspects of our existence and nature that we can create a more balanced understanding of our purpose. Lying creates confusion and is a function of the basic instinct, and is at the negative end of the spectrum of the

Dichotic Dilemma. The truth creates understanding and a platform for reasoned logic as a basis for understanding the more difficult aspects about that truth. It is appealing to our higher function and at the positive end of the spectrum of the Dichotic Dilemma. Positively dealing with the challenges that the truth can cause is the way to create balance, a balanced understanding and perspective.

1.9 "We are trapped and enslaved by this modernity that shackles us in its, and with its, very essence.
This is preposterous?
If it is indeed preposterous to you, that is a very sure sign and indicator of the truth in the statement."

This piece of writing is in response to the difficulties associated with modern living. However, by virtue of the Dichotic Dilemma, every possible system of existence will have its difficulties. The difficulties are brought on by the need to survive and the way in which we go about ensuring the state of that survival, determines how we experience life. Through the transition of time, humanity is now at a stage where every aspect of trade is balanced against a monetary value. On this basis, money becomes the functional conduit towards living life in the way one wants, or being subject to the constraints and limitations of not having money.

The limitations of this system are that money becomes the centre of human existence and such a scenario means that humanity's main point of focus is money. Money is the means to survival. Consequently, the effect is that human existence is then being governed by the dictates of our lesser selves, the dictates of the survival instinct. Hence, notions such as, "if it makes money it makes sense" arise and such a concept in many ways functions in spite of the ramifications of social consequence. It promotes the dominance of the more negative attributes of the human survival instinct which can be played out to the extremes. Self-interest, moral vacuity and such notions can percolate into all aspects of human societal existence. Moral and social dilemmas are less significant when weighed up against the profit motive.

Being raised as a Christian, one of the teachings from the bible which always rings true to myself is that, the love of money is the root of all evil. I qualify this again by stating that, functionally, being overly money-oriented is appealing to the basic survival instinct. Humanity transforms into extremes of hunter and hunted, predators and prey, and the function becomes survival of the fittest.

Of course, the monetary system has its advantages as it creates incentive. However, it is a system that requires heavy moral input and balancing because it is a very functional system which can turn human existence into being just about survival. Indeed, survival is a fundamental input to our existence. However, the challenge is, as human beings with our relatively greater faculties, can we aspire to be more?

On that basis, writing becomes a very important and powerful medium of expression as ideas can be discussed in the context of freedom of speech which is a very liberating and powerful phenomenon when implemented positively. Hence, with my freedom of speech, I will say this:

Is it so farfetched to envisage a world devoid of the concept of money as we know it today?

Existing under the current monetary system encourages exploitation with inevitable social stratification leaving others poor, others desperately so, and destitute, with all the resultant social ramifications which lead to a very negative perception of our existence. We live in a world of nano-technology, extraordinary technological sophistication, yet our social existence is still nigh on barbaric observed as a collective. Are we not intelligent enough to create a system whereby we embrace a collective humanity and do away with arbitrary lines which mean, instead of existing together on this planet, we grab, fight and steal from each other? Exploit each other and the planet? This is a juxtaposition that brings into clear light the extremes of the ramifications of the Dichotic

Dilemma. A potential greatness lost by appealing to the dictates of our lesser selves, our basic instinct, our infantile state as a species of beings. We have gone through the Stone Age, the Iron Age and so on, leading up to now, an age of extremely advanced technology in relative terms. Can our social existence not reflect this advancement as well?

By and large, by great forces, some explained and some still unknown or unproven, we as human beings lived quite separately in seemingly distinct and disparate groups. We have intermingled through the ages, however, not as pointedly and as forcibly as we do today by virtue of technology and expanding population levels, which brings us closer.

Through subsequent interaction, we realise, we are not that different and, fundamentally, we are the same. Hence, just as an idea, perchance a farfetched one, can the process which has brought us to this point through fighting, war and hate, lesser emotional and human functions. Can it not be the process which, as akin to growing pains, be the process that gives rise to a new human civilisation, a collective form of existence? Or are we too subject to the dictates of our lesser selves, our basic instinct? The Dichotic Dilemma. The mind believes what it is told and shown.

A personal belief is to hold true that some things must be said, whether to fall on deaf ears and be ineffectual, as long as they have been said.

1.10 "The secret to life is attaining a balance.
We have a great teacher, The EARTH we inhabit.
As we are some of its inhabitants, we have to live
by its rules and we are bound by them.
If you push here, it will have an effect there, force and
effect, simple physics, an invariable consequence.
Therefore, in everything you do, you have to attain a balance.
If we over exploit and pollute the environment,
it is only to our own eventual detriment.

Address the balance, every action has a reaction. So do not push
too hard if you do not want the object you push to go too far.
Do not take too much, everything in moderation.
Give things time to recover.
You should be gradual.
Do not go too close to the sun, for it is too hot, do
not go too far from the sun, for it is too cold.
Measure your actions, have caution.
Know what you are doing and why you do it and
Account for any possible reverberations.
What you cannot understand, only meddle in when
you understand it or can cope with any potential
consequences, be they desirable or adverse.
If you have nothing to say, do not speak, else sound like a fool.
Do not be too loud or too quiet.
Respect the balance because the earth,
our mother shows us how to.
However, some do not know this truth, their
greatest mistake was to think they knew.
A mind that is convinced it knows all cannot learn.
For how can you search if you think you have found it?
How can you thirst if you believe your thirst is quenched?
Be humble and you will be raised, you can only
go up if you have been down and if you are up
or think you are up, you can only go down.
Those are the laws of nature, that's what
our mother permits us to do.
But we have been taught to ignore her, turn a blind eye
when she cries or her belly rumbles because she is sick
of the poison she ingests on account of our actions.
Or when she gets hot or parched as she thirsts
for the life essence that is being drained away from her.

When she weeps, we weep, for she is our mother.
Those who revel in her pain and don't feel her pain
when she is in pain are not her children.
They are invaders, intruders who will rape her, not suckle
from her bosom as she cares for her children. But brutalise
her, take from her children, torture her family and profit and
make merry from her suffering and her children's suffering.
We are the children of the earth, she is our mother.
We have failed her, now we seek for
answers...........
The answers are in ourselves.
True freedom is not given or bought, it is earned.
And in this time, it is only through the blood,
sweat and the tears of many tortured souls.
Till that day, we shall plead, beg and suffer.
Open your eyes sons and daughters of the mother.
The mother who blessed, nurtured and made you. Wake up,
wake up for she weeps now, wake up before it is too late.
Wake up before this malice, this pestilence, this cancer
becomes malignant and there is nothing to save.
Wake up before you really are dead.
For you are more than dead right now,
you are worse than dead.
Wake up children, wake up. Your mother weeps, wake up.

The piece is abstract and is characterised in part by political overtones. Visions of exploitative raiders and invaders which is in reference to the process of colonisation in Africa by Western powers and the subsequent exploitation of the earth and those colonised. Colonisation however, is a process that has existed in history between groups irrespective of racial lines as the groups struggled for survival, dominance, and resources. The ongoing story and struggle for survival.

However, more pointedly in this instance, this piece is relating to the exploitation of the earth for profit and some of its views echo the piece and extrapolation immediately preceding it. The question being, should we exploit the earth, its flora and fauna for mindless profit or use what we should and must to necessitate our existence and the resultant existential political and social systems that would result from each proposed paradigm of existence?

There are some people who perceive the earth from a spiritual perspective and speak of a symbiosis between us as humanity on the earth and the earth itself, the flora and fauna. Certainly it is a perspective worth noting because by its very nature, it encourages a sustainable existence. The way that the dominating nations exist at the moment and the ensuing direction they have taken, the human race is generally agreed not to be sustainable. Yet, the mechanics of that existence are embedded into every aspect of modern day living. The interesting observation to note however, is that, certainly, intrinsic observation reveals that, where we are at this stage, was not a matter of pure choice. However, more a reflection of the human story as human beings tried to understand who we are and also answer the challenges of survival, leading eventually, through discovery and technological advancement to the current status quo. The civilisations that have powered our arrival to modern day existence were victims of design; necessity leading to technological development in the name of trying to improve the state of existence. Yet now humanity seems subject to the system it has created. Leading to rising population levels and depleting natural resources. All factors will lead to more strife as we continue to live as different geopolitical entities trying to survive individually in a volatile and challenging world.

Yet, seemingly arguing for a monoculture and singular understanding and perspective appears to be against what we value as human beings; our different identities and our different cultures. I will argue that culture is something that develops as a group of human beings occupies a particular geographical area over a period of time creating identity and traits that distinguish that particular group. Yet, in the grandest observation of life, humanity, and our existence (our collective existence) is a phenomenon that transcends time and space and is exponentially more of a fantastic observation than the traits of a single group's culture. On the grandest observation of life, I would ask, which is more important and edifying to value, our individual tribalistic and territorial values or the collective value of the human race? As ever, The Dichotic Dilemma, the fabric of life.

Yet, as we struggle with and ponder on life's complications and complexities, its complex beauty, and more uplifting aspects are ever present, even if just for a flicker. Hence, for those who appreciate the expressions of the emotional state, I will encourage them to enjoy, if not just appreciate, the ensuing poem.

1.11 "I love you. I hope our wounds can heal so that we can cherish this beautiful love we have found in this land
of hurt and pain.
Times together are heaven itself.
For only heaven can be that beautiful.
You are my angel sent from the heavens to help me
along this journey, let's not let ourselves down.
You are beautiful, and so is this love.
My heart beats for you, I breathe for you, I wake up for you.
Let's make it grow.
That's my greatest and most precious of wishes.
We need the trust so that those that would tear
us asunder can have no say in our bond.
We should love and respect each other for love is a precious
yet dangerous gift and you have to know how to cherish it.
When it is true, its essence should and will guide you.
It's time to grow. my passion."

Chapter Two!!

"True Brave Is Doing The Right Thing When You Are Most Scared."

2.1 "A true leader is a leader who stands for the weak.
For his job is to defend those who are
defenceless by their own devices.
The strong do not need any protection, for by their
very nature, they can protect themselves.
Therefore, in a pack, a true leader is he who walks
at the back of the herd with the weak and wounded
and protects them from the predators that lurk in
the dark waiting to pounce on the failing, for a
predator thrives on weakness.
The strong will find their way home but the
weak need guidance and protection.
Thus from this the leader grows in stature and
becomes a stronger and an ever more magnanimous
figure amongst those who stand alongside him".

Leadership and power: the most defining factors to how we experience our existence as human beings here on this planet. The analogies are endless, but certainly, the leader represents the head, the brain. What the brain commands and demands, the rest of the body is subject to it and obeys. Translated into the human social sphere, this function becomes an issue of great contention as many become subject to one or a few.

As an observation however, I see the poem naturally assumes a leader as a he or male. This is reflective of the concepts and notions I grew up around and certainly, the conflict between the roles of the genders. I believe in the value of the idea and I believe in coexistence and relativity as the functions that should govern role-play in life between genders. Only a woman can give birth to a child and only a man can sire children in the strictest terms. These are biological dictates. However, beyond that, relativity abounds as to what function should be played by which gender and this I believe should be the defining ethos of 21st century thinking. Behaviour and practice should be based on the best idea, and where that idea comes from, at best is a function of natural selection. Hence, all should be respected and afforded due right to propose a valid idea despite outward presentation. The human being is far more than we can comprehend with our naked eye.

Certainly, this idea is most poignant within the realms of leadership, power, and dominance. Through the ages, humanity has faced strife on account of the actions of those who have found themselves as leaders. Tales of Vlad the Impaler, Kings and Emperors, Pharaohs and Chiefs who were Gods on earth able to take or spare life at a whim and flicker of emotion. In some parts of the world, there has been a transition away from these extremes of governance by and large, yet, many parts of the world are still subject to tyranny and political strife. It is difficult to think of a place on earth with a perfect model, however, it is fair to say that areas where there is stability and relative plenty, more stable political systems exist. Where humanity has addressed the basic survival need for food, higher function has been attained technologically and politically.

On that basis, naturally, ensuring these factors globally should realise more stable political systems. How, though, as a species do we arrive at this stage when the variables that can confound such a process are innumerable and seem impossible to overcome? Jingoism, self- protectionism, greed, hate, difference, historical imbalances, unrepresentative political systems, ignorance, flawed routes to power and a myriad other factors. How do we arrive at a stage where we can elect credible representative leaders with grand ideas that can truly uplift the collective state of our race? We certainly need a shift in perspective as a species, as a humanity as the fore occupiers of this realm of existence.

2.2 "In this life, we have to be strong, so strong that
sometimes we are embarrassed to be weak or show weakness
to the point that we become cold and cold-hearted.
However, you can only get strong or stronger
if you have been weak or weaker.
So cry, show your weakness, for there is love and compassion
to be found in weakness and strength to be gained.
For we are but human, thus we are not impregnable
to forces that can prevail over us at times.
It is this understanding of ourselves we need.
We are subject to those stronger than us and
they owe us a debt of gratitude.
For it is in our weakness that they are stronger.
The greatest knowledge is understanding of self."

A show of oppressive strength is a survival instinct. A need to show dominance in an effort to ensure one's own survival and superiority. It is a basic function, an animalistic function and response to adversity and the challenges of survival. Within the animal kingdom, the weak are preyed on and that is the law of nature and how survival and balance are maintained within that paradigm of existence. Such analogies exist within the human social sphere of existence and are and have been expressed through the ages. So when we fight, we are as animals because we are incapable of applying the functions of higher understanding to reach a solution and an outcome.

I believe in true strength being the strength of character. Strength of character is based on deep understanding and attributes which appeal to our higher function and the capabilities of the mind applied positively. Strength of character is a rational function requiring rational input and temperance. This is real strength, true strength that is constructive, cohesive, and balanced as we use higher function to see through the plight of our existence as opposed to more basic actions such as oppressive shows of strength.

Relating to the previous idea of leadership, an abundance of these attributes in those who lead us would see more positive outcomes within our sphere of existence. Overcoming the challenges of our existence through understanding and balance is a functional tool towards a better existence.

Yet often, strength and power are shown oppressively by human beings. Particularly amongst those who lead us or come to lead us more often than not. This by the virtue of the process of power where a human being is valued beyond balance and their influence is over extended. The mind perceives this and can consequently create any conceptualisation of the meaning of that power which can have positive or negative effects on the rest by virtue of the dominant characteristics of the individual, whether positive or negative. The corrupting influence of power. Hence, Monarchies, Emperors, Dictators, Rulers, those with that authority can consequently instil any oppressive forms of government on their people. This idea transcends existence to even micro interactions in work, in the home, through life, and social existence as the notion of strength and power that is emphasised oppressively or negatively.

Strength of mind, strength of character, the power of understanding and the devolution of power. No one person is all things. That is the function of collective human existence. The amalgamation of disparate perspectives harmoniously through understanding.

These are the functional inputs of strength and power that can contribute to a more balanced human existence. A lion with the same mouth it uses to devour and predate prey, also can carry its cubs and hold them gently within its mighty fangs. The Dichotic Dilemma. We present differently in myriad forms, some weak, some strong in any respect. There is a function to this and this is what necessitates social stratification so that each aspect of survival can be seen through the input of the collective. If everyone is the same, then the diversity needed to fulfil different social functions is not present. Each is valuable in spite of their seemingly weak or lesser position relative to others.

You cannot have the whole without the sum of its parts. Understanding the necessity of others, however they present, is the function of a greater understanding. Those who by the virtue of natural selection gain the fortune of finding themselves in dominance over others should always know that their power is by the virtue of the presence of others. We need to develop strength in the powers of understanding and not strength in the powers of oppression. We need to gain power in understanding how to apply the influence of power and limit its corrupting influence.

We as human beings can communicate vocally more intricately and diversely than the other creatures on this planet. Are we incapable of using this ability to live through our disparities in a positive and balanced way? Indeed again, we need a shift in perspective.

2.4 "I must either be stupid or really love you.
Because you have taken away so much
of my honour and dignity.
I pray, there are better days ahead for today I feel a great pain.
Why do you not consider me in your actions, do
you not know my affections are with you?
It is not ignorance the way you act, it is crudeness and rudeness.
I am not a man, I am a fool, for a man would never
stand and bear witness to your actions.
I have ceased to be a man, for all my pride and
dignity has been stripped from me whilst I stood
and watched without moving a muscle except
the muscle that moved as my heart broke.

*However, I am not just a man, I am more
than a man, for a normal man sees what is in
front of him and takes it as the truth.
But I am the man to see what is behind it and beyond.
For a person's action is not but an action. It is a combination
of their experiences, interpretations and understanding.
You have broken my heart, and broken it again, and yet again.
However, you have not known. So for this reason, I forgive you.
For as much as I have loved you, your love for me
has grown in return.
Ignorance is not an excuse, but because I LOVE
YOU, and I know you now, I forgive you.
For only you can mend my heart, you own
it. It is yours to keep and take care of.
As I heal the wounds of my broken heart and
pray they heal, I pray the scars build a layer
so strong it can never be broken again.
I hope you can begin to fathom the task
that lies ahead of you. I love you.
Make me happy, make me a happy man, for I love
you."*

As ever, we always come back to the concept of love. Great power is to be found in this notion. As expressed before, this power can breed positive outcomes, or it can breed negative outcomes relative to circumstance. However, as expressed coming to the end of the poem, through the power of understanding, the young man sees through his pain and realises a better perspective through the turmoil of life and ignorance. Understanding is what breeds harmony in love; equally, understanding is what breeds harmony in life.

*2.4 "You should never forget. Forgive but never forget.
Everything you go through is your guide.*

*A catalogue of events that show you what
is right and what is wrong.
That made you happy, that made you sad.
If you forget, you are bound to repeat what
you have done because that is where your
fundamental human nature guides you.
Learn from your mistakes for you are doomed to
repeat what you do not endeavour to never repeat."*

Through the ages, and today, as we continue to exist through time, we exist as disparate entities. We have waged war and killed one another since time immemorial, the victors enjoying dominance and the spoils of victory. At times unspeakable acts of severe brutality have been committed as we wage war because war and fighting shifts to an extreme, a negative extreme that is perceived as right or wrong. Killing becomes normal and methods of killing arise, each as dastardly as the other and some worse. Biological warfare, germ warfare, unspeakable instruments of death which at times have ramifications that echo far into the distant future through their negative effect. Ramifications of the basic survival instinct expressed through our higher functioning minds completely degrades what we are and can be as human beings. This distorts the balance in our collective existential plane and brings to light the extremes of the Dichotic Dilemma. Others have been enslaved and risen against their captors in a never-ending cycle of human existence. The same story repeated is in different situations throughout time, throughout the world; an oppressive power and leadership that confounds a greater understanding through time in the name of survival.

However, time heals all and what happened before can and is forgotten through the renewal of generations and changing societal dynamics in different geographical locations. Yet, human nature stays the same. Our fundamental state and requirements stay the same; the need to survive.

Consequently, we are doomed to repeat what we have done before if we do not always look back in history to learn from our mistakes.

Genocides, mass murder, oppression, and slavery are all part of our past, present and future if we do not learn from the past and negate our lesser selves. This is why pain is a teacher. Through suffering, understanding can be gained by observing the factors that contributed to that suffering. Bringing balance to a once unbalanced state. This also is the power of forgiveness, on the basis that forgiveness is a function of understanding. Looking through the actions of the transgressor, understanding their motivations, learning from them and moving on positively and constructively with the knowledge gained from the pain.

Forgiving is of more use to the transgressed because they carry the pain. Forgiving someone is a function of self-empowerment as it allows the transgressed to relieve themselves of the pain inflicted through understanding. As long as you hold on to the pain and anger, you stay at that stage and gain nothin; only potentially a need for revenge which, yes, can be a way to readdress the balance but in a negative way. Forgiveness, a concept that transcends every aspect of human social existence, is an ideal that requires and asks the utmost of ourselves, an appeal to a higher function. An edifying concept, a unifying concept, and an exercise in the functionality of understanding ignorance and pain.

Forgive but never forget. Balance and understanding. An appeal to our greater selves. The power of understanding.

2.6 *"Writing is a catharsis.*
There are over five billion people on this earth, but we
are really alone.
We are alone in our experience and we are
alone in our perception of experience.
For every little thing that happens, the whole world could
see it, but it have a completely differing and sometimes
absolutely opposite meaning to someone standing next to you.
Therefore, at times people can fail to understand you

no matter how much you strive to explain yourself.
Hence, a pen will follow and the page will absorb
and they will never question or oppose.
Thus you ventilate, you ventilate, and you ventilate.
Hello paper, hello pen, hello friend.
What a catharsis."

In many ways, this piece is about the power of positive expression. Fighting oppression poses many dilemmas. How do you depose violent oppressive overloads with just words and non-violent protest? The power of the bullet, machete or bayonet is immediately more decisive than the power of the pen and the voice. How do you reason with a tyrant and tyrannical governments or overloads when reason is not their language of choice? How do you challenge ignorance when its natural inclination is towards a violent response? The function of unbalanced minds.

If someone is bent on oppressing you, how do just words release you from your burden? Yet the most celebrated freedom fighters were those who chose non-violent protest in the face of the gravest tyranny. Martin Luther King Junior, Mahatma Gandhi, and as the Bible has it, Jesus Christ. Their message became the more edifying and uplifting one for humanity. Some died in the effort, a lesson through pain. The young student in Tiananmen Square. A gripping insight and vivid observation into the gravity of the fight against the tyranny that power can impose. A lone human being standing against the full might of oppressive power. A vivid and striking insight into the manifestation of the Dichotic Dilemma at its most extreme in the human sphere of existence. Ever more so, indeed as I type, 2011 has witnessed what is being termed the Arab Spring. A rise against the mechanisms of power in that region which has shown that fundamentally, we all want the same thing, to be able to fend for loved ones in a stable environment. We should harness these moments and such lessons as the symbol of what to aspire to as the future continually beckons. Always being wary as ever of the power of the mechanics that can cause division and oppression.

That is the power of positive expression, understanding what drives those who are called terrorists by others to acts of extreme retaliation. Nelson Mandela was once called a terrorist. The question should be, what makes a so-called terrorist a terrorist? Violence is a negative and basic expression of frustration but in an unbalanced imperfect world, as long as we live divided as a species, the function of division can lead to extremes and extremes of violence. Another person's terrorist is another person's freedom fighter. The Dichotic Dilemma.

I, too, was frustrated at the world one day by no design of my own. Writing came naturally to me by virtue of my nature and my surroundings. Other people face harsher challenges and are then prone to more severe pathways of expressing their frustration. However, ultimately, my position is forever a stand for non-violence, to aspire for something more. Nothing happens by coincidence.
Balance, understanding, and forgiveness.

To find balance, we need to address the mechanisms of power and the mechanisms of leadership in our world. Opinion is powered by perspective. We need a new perspective as we pursue the demands of our survival.

2.7 "How can I not love you?
For you are a blessing sent from above in answer to a
solitary prayer uttered long ago on a cold and
starry night as I lay in a lonely bed.
A blessing from the heavens sent to bring happiness
to me even in my coldest and darkest hour.
For your smile and the warmth gained from your tender
bosom is enough to melt away even the saddest of thoughts.
However, such a treasure cannot just be
received, it has to be earned.
For what is good is worth fighting for and waiting
for."

Emotions: the colour of human existence.

2.8 "The world we live in today is teaching us to be lazy.
Every technological advancement is teaching us not
only to be lazy, but to do exactly what the system wants
us to do and that is essentially to get stuck in
the rat race for that is how the system sustains itself.
And the biggest sloth machine is the television. Grown people
sit and stir at it for hours on end as it lies and transmits
images to convince us that we are looking at real people.
Not only are the transmissions just electronic
Impulses, the people in the television are also
inventions, caricatures, characters in a play.
As we continue to gaze into the mechanical
box, we disconnect from real people.
Our mothers, fathers, brothers and sisters and remain
gazing into this fantasy machine as it continues
to delude us, and we lose track of reality and
have no time for what really matters in life.
The result is an insensitive, emotionally, challenged,
mechanical and vacuous society where whole
generations are being raised by a machine as their
guardians toil for the proverbial paycheque.
Trapped we are.
Break free we must."

This piece is struggling to deal with a lot of issues at the same time. There is a mention of technology, which as we know it today has had a tremendous impact on human existence and in many ways how we define ourselves. Mentioned in the poem is a perception of some of the societal impacts of this technology against the more wholesome aspects of human existence. Indeed as well, present is the mention of money and the monetary system which is seen as a slave master.

As discussed before, money has been referenced as the extension of the struggle to survive being played out in a different paradigm. We have always been subject to the need to survive and each mode of existence has had its benefits and demerits. However, most pointedly in this piece, is the mention of technology.

Every action has a reaction. In the same vein, every technological advance has a determinant consequence on human social existence either positive or negative by virtue of the Dichotic Dilemma. At the earlier stages of modern-day technological advancement, social consequence was realised or considered after the effects of the technology had been realised. Consequently, in the 21st century, we have problems with pollution, environmental degradation, waste disposal, and general resource wastage. Hence, the definite challenge is, how do we balance out this equation? In essence, technological ingenuity is a human urge to try and avail or answer life's survival questions. In its most basic form, it involved stone tools moving on to where we are now in the 21st century.

We seem to be at a stage where we have harnessed and are in control of the understanding needed to manipulate the elements for our benefit. Consequently, technology in some respects is ceasing to be an answer to necessity. Hence it seems, at this stage, technology has become less in answer on the social scale to our needs but more to our wants with obvious social disparities and consequences a factor in this equation. As need is resolved, only want remains with seemingly limitless progression and consequently, we are now progressing to an extreme that creates waste mainly powered by the dictates of the profit motive. Certainly, the benefits are of constantly improving technology on an exponential scale. Computers now have capabilities that go beyond what they could do less than a decade ago. Powered by the ability to build on already-existing knowledge and on that analysis by the virtue of where technology is now, the possibilities and limits are endless.

The question is, what are the potential social costs and impacts of this exponential progression in a very short space of time relatively? Are we on the course for another Hiroshima moment where the confluence of all that had been learnt became a deathly spectre? Certainly, if our technological progression is powered by the force of negative factors, greed, war, hate and the thirst for power, money and profit, the prospects of the effect of technology on our social existence could be dim. Unfortunately, in life, we are at the mercy of hindsight. Hence, the need for caution, wise judgement, and guidance in the decision-making process, especially the things that will affect us the most. We need to harness the power of technology for the good of all human beings and not just through the power of poorly guided ambitions and abilities. As long as the factors driving us the most are governed by the need for profit, then we might only be going on a path where we rue the consequences and forever cry about social injustice and the malice of existence.

Technological advancement in the 21st century has given human beings great power indeed. The power to create, control and manipulate, some say, the power to play God. That is great power indeed for humanity's ability in the 21st century to manipulate the elements is truly phenomenal. Wireless connectivity, satellites orbiting the earth, and a myriad of other advances affecting 21st-century existence. Yet power, any power, but as in this instance, power of this magnitude is that thing that can either be most beneficial or most destructive in the hands of human beings who are, as it has been said, part angel and part ape.

In nature, all things that grow uncontrollably or react to an extreme are of ill consequence to the environment around them. We are part of nature and are governed by its laws, and at times, we find out to our peril. We have had centuries of fighting and learning from pain and living disparately to learn from. Yet, with the 21st century presenting humanity with the most momentous of challenges and opportunity, can we live as one? Technology allows us to be closer than we have ever been and see through our disparities. The collisions of civilisations under tumultuous circumstances have inadvertently brought us closer together and, through social progression and time, forced us to live together. An ongoing human social experiment. When the first Westerners arrived and founded their colonies and raped, in some instances, the indigenous women, some of them started to fear what they were creating, "mixed race people". Yet, what emerged were human beings proving that the differences were only superficial. Humanity is intrinsic, intrinsic in all of us.

We have a dark history of social learning as we have struggled to survive and are always at each other's proverbial throats. Through it all, we have a catalogue of learning against our lesser selves through history as we suffer from the effect of the influence of our lesser selves and the carnage we can cause as yes, indeed, we are the masters of this plane through our multitude.

In the 21st century, we have an opportunity to bring this pain all together and learn from it with the aim of a better existence powered by the power of technology. Ethics, Human Rights, the United Nations, the International Monetary Fund, and other bodies. All incomplete attempts at trying to unify a disparate humanity and save it from its lesser self. Incomplete because there are still disparities in how the benefits and influence of these ideals and bodies are applied globally. We still need further political, social, and economic evolution, if not revolution and progress, before the benefits of these ideals can be of benefit to all. Nothing happens by coincidence, but we can learn from our mistakes. Past strife has laid the foundation, but can we meet the challenge?

Technology is an attempt to answer life's question of survival. We seem to have harnessed its power, now an opportunity presents itself for it to be used for universal benefit. Yet, the Dichotic Dilemma is an ever- present force as we seek to attain and understand the power of balance. To understand the importance of the one against the many and the many against one. We have an opportunity and technology is the key, the answer to the question of survival. Can we harness its power positively? Our final evolutionary step.

2.9 *"How can you fight for your freedom when you are not*

being oppressed?
How can you defend yourself if you are not being attacked?
How can you go and cleanse someone else's house
when your own is extremely dirty?
How can you move a nation to go and correct the
"mistakes" of others when you have not looked within
yourself to find the mistakes that are in you?
How can you fight in the name of the
Righteous one when you shun him, laugh
at him and act against his will?
Are you really fighting for the truth and
justice you preach or is this your mask?
Is this the mask you wear to fool those who you have
"blessed" with ignorance so that they do not see your
truly ugly face and be revolted by it?
You can fool them, but you cannot fool me.
I see through you because I look at you
through the eyes of knowledge.
RIGHT KNOWLEDGE.
Your time will come to pass, so toil, toil, toil
for redemption and salvation shall prevail one
day for this is the law of the cosmos."

Growing up, I believed in strict right and wrong, good and evil, and equally so, good and evil people. When you are young, in many ways, this is the concept of existence you are taught and ultimately, being raised as a Christian, this is the concept I was taught. However, as I have grown older, I have realised a different perspective. I have realised relativity and that the concept of good and evil does not fully account for wider and more intrinsic variables which contribute to human existence.

Consequently, believing in good and evil makes it very easy for others to become hypocrites, liars, sinners, the damned and condemned, essentially, evil people, by virtue of their actions as one perceives them.

On that basis, this poem is in response to people I saw as evil at the time, the Great Western Hoards. They seemed to be hypocritical in their rhetoric of defending themselves when in my view, they were quite clearly the oppressors. The visions of white oppressive dominance, which I grew up observing in my country of origin Zimbabwe, and particularly South Africa, America and Europe, claimed to be God-fearing Christians. The same observation I was making as America seemed to drop bombs on other nations and with my own Zimbabwean colonial history vivid in my consciousness. Yet the rhetoric was that these actions were in self-defence of God-fearing Christians, and it was by His might and right they were carried out.

Yet, this rhetoric is not only endemic to Western civilisations, some who follow Islam and other beliefs, justify their behaviour in the same way. However, more so, the perceived function of hypocrisy is present even in interpersonal human interactions. Summed up as, do as I say, not as I do. Hence, trying to figure out the truth and a moral standard against this backdrop from an indoctrinated religious perspective powered this piece, highlighting to me today again, the power of perspective and how polarising it can be with all the resultant consequences. Hence, the proposal of The Dichotic Dilemma, within the human social sphere of existence is powered by our higher functioning minds underpinned by survival instinct. Equally, and more so, is the need for understanding and appreciation of the power of balance in the light of grander observations and possibilities.

This is the power of perspective, a quantum shift, and human social evolution.

2.10 "The deepest meaning is in simplicity.
FUNDAMENTALS and PRINCIPLES.
The beginning is where the answer to all problems lies.
However, we manage to complicate what is simple.
Thus through the turmoil and confusion that results
from the complications, we manage to lose track

of what is right and just, and what is wrong and folly. The deepest meaning is in simplicity.
These are the building blocks of "CIVILISATION."

I believe in intrinsic observation powered by universal principles. Logical deduction is the power of universal understanding, a fundamental understanding, reductionism to a point source creating the basis for a greater awareness. It is called science, but in essence, it is a human function only now it is applied under well-established protocols creating a functional standardised appreciation of the function of rational thinking. However, it is certainly a human function whose same principles can also be used to advance human social existence by virtue of understanding who and what we are in a reductionist manner. An earthly being with distinct input characteristics which define who and what we are as existential beings.

In social terms, we are more engaged with addressing the symptoms of what we are and on this basis, we stand against each other. We observe our differences and create labels based on the perceived social norms of different societies and cultures. Yet, if we go back far enough, it is clear to see that we originate from a singular source, the deepest meaning is in simplicity, the building blocks of civilisation.

Understanding and applying simple ideas positively under a universal system is true human civilisation. All faiths propose the same core principles, yet it is the matters beyond the principles that seem to dictate most how the people in those faiths act. Respect your fellow human being. A simple idea, with the most profound meaning, a universal teaching. The power of simplicity, the atom, the cell, the simplest structures, the most profound consequence. Existence. The power of simplicity, an understanding which dictates the realisation of greater possibilities.

2.11 "Everything that is, was meant to be because everything that is, is designed to result in the way things are.
Very simple but yet very complex. The

deepest meaning is in simplicity.
This is why we always have to look back in
history because this is where the answers to
everything lie. For this is where it started.
This is why the black man has to learn his
history, HIS STORY, HIS TRUTH.
For this is his only salvation and that is the only way
he will ever know himself and why he suffers so
dearly."

I believe in determinism. However, free will certainly is free will but it is still a relative and predetermined function. In this way again, it is possible to negate the notion of good and evil. I do not refute that "bad" or "evil" things certainly do happen, however I prefer the term negative as it refers to the idea of balance. "Bad" or "evil" is a matter of perspective as white people, for example, do not see themselves as evil in the context of the colonisation and subjugation of other races in recent history. Rather, as conquerors, and explorers and yes they enjoy the spoils by and large. Hence, as we have already established, the need for understanding and always appreciating the input function of the survival instinct in the human social equation.

Hence, as a black man, in the poem, I called for the black race to learn from history as a way to restore the balance of the oppression the race has faced in recent history and, in many ways, still faces today through the residual effects of colonisation and slavery. For the purpose of gaining a functional understanding of causality that replaces hurt and pain with constructive knowledge.

However, again, I have asserted that I believe in determinism. In principle, if you put any human being under the same conditions, you generally will get the same results. Relativity is a factor, but in the strictest terms, the assertion stands. For example, if an Indian baby is raised in Scotland, that baby will sound like a Scot. If any human being is put in a deprived environment without a way out, they will most inevitably be reduced to the lesser means of ensuring their survival. If a child is raised to believe a certain idea or ideology, they will most likely believe and live by it. If you are trained to kill, you will kill. Your environment, by and large, determines what you believe and how you act. Determinism. Again yes, relativity is a factor but again, in the strictest terms, the assertion stands. Hence, there is an input function to every individual's behaviour across the spectrum from positive to negative. Moreover, to understand each individual's behaviour is to retrace them to the point of inception and therein lies every individual. A simple idea with complex ramifications to our social existence which leads ultimately to the idea of God or the creator. If determinism is a function of human existence then ultimately, something must have determined this existence. We will revisit the idea of God further along the way.

2.12 "You rush to point out what others can and cannot do.
However, when you do wrong, you think it is your prerogative. Your mandate.
You look down on and mock good honourable people when you have no shred of honour or dignity. Yet you are "above" me and I have no "power" over you and you get "everything" without trying.
And you hate my success when I bleed and scratch and sweat for it.
Yet, I do not hate you, and that is the strangest thing.
I hate your ways and I pity you.
Yet you hate me when I have never wronged you."

Human existence poses many social dilemmas which make us question the necessity of our very existence on occasion. Little wonder some look up to the sky always and ask why!

This piece is the voice of a young teenage boy who finds himself in a strange and different land all of a sudden, and is altogether engulfed by the malice of xenophobia, hate and ignorance. It is the voice of the underprivileged immigrant. The hate for foreigners is an intrinsic survival response.

An immigrant, strictly speaking, is an individual who goes to a new environment seeking better prospects. It is a natural response to an antagonistic and malnourished environment. Yet in the human social sphere, it is an issue of great contention as tribalism and territorialism induce a natural mal-response to the idea of an immigrant exacerbated by the function of difference. Indeed, looking historically with reference to tribal infighting, village infighting, and marauding armies hacking and slashing their way through kingdoms and homesteads. Savage world wars, tribal wars, racial wars. Outsiders potentially pose a threat to existence and what a group values in every way; physical existence, culture, beliefs, and most importantly, resources. Hence, it is not surprising to see why the idea of outsiders can provoke at times a violent fearful response. The response is ingrained into the subconscious, an intrinsic survival response, an animalistic response.

However, we purport to be better than and above the animals. At least, it can be argued that animals know no better. We should be able to overcome our animalistic responses in light of a grander inclusive vision.

In the 21st century, we need to harness the power of the idea of the human being. We live in a world where it seems acceptable and the norm that others have absolutely nothing and other billionaires. We have accepted third worlds, ghettos, and squalor as though we are unaware of the contributing factors to such a reality. A chronic imbalance in the distribution of resources creates an endless stream of economic migrants to those places where wealth is centred. It is logical enough to conclude that a more equitable redistribution of wealth, education, and resources would abate such a situation. To harness the power and efficacy of meritocracy and individualism against the needs and presence of the wider society.

I argue that it is not that resources are limited on this planet, rather, they are mismanaged by virtue of the influence of unbalanced ideals. We need to reinvent the wheel, the function of the equitable redistribution of resources. We need to harness the power of the idea of the human being. Wisdom to our leaders, wisdom to our leaders.

2.13 "The difference between black people and every other
race is that we are not united under one ideology,
and most importantly, our own ideology.
We all think differently thus we do not have accord
without which, the result is that we can never
stand together as one force.
We do not share a common knowledge anymore, a
common knowledge and a common understanding.
Our minds are polluted and brainwashed with
a knowledge which is foreign to us.
As one great black man once said, "We have become so
much like the white man such that we think it absurd when
someone tries to teach us and tell us about ourselves."

Once, I was engrossed with the plight of my race alone and only identified with and sort to understand and address that plight. Yet now, I identify with the human plight, the universal human plight in the fight to survive. And fight we do indeed when we could collaborate powered by our differences and universal similarities. Mustard gas, stealth bombers, cluster bombs, weapons of mass destruction, and now we have the Atomic bomb. Who are we fighting against and killing? I would argue, we are killing ourselves.

Who are we so afraid of and trying to kill as we arm ourselves to the teeth whilst playing who has the biggest stick with nuclear weapons? We are all human beings, and the biggest threat to our survival is not living by that ideal and consequently being destroyed by our own actions as has been the case throughout history and does not look to be

The Dichotic Dilemma

abating. What does it say about what we are as supposedly intelligent existential beings when we cannot see past the superficiality of our differences? Are we so governed by our basic instincts that we cannot exist harmoniously as a collective beyond the dictates of these lesser urges? Our urges to dominate, and at times ultimately kill, to necessitate our survival over others. We are our own greatest enemy, threat, and fear through ignorance.

If we do not learn from history, the future looks bleak.

A lot of forward thinkers through the ages have described dystopian apocalyptic visions of the future based on their assessment of our nature against prevailing and potential societal trends. Of course, those are only perspectives but their function is to warn us against our lesser nature. At times, faced by the mundane nature of day-to-day existence as the days roll by, it is difficult to appreciate the effect of grander consequences until they arise.

Indeed, through pain we learn. Have we not by now learnt our lesson?

2.14 "You should not be an idealist, rather you should be a realist with ideals.
For it is ideals that create such phenomena as racism
and movements like the eugenics movement.
For someone who is idealistic will try to
mould the world to his ideal.
"HITLER".
However, a realist will acknowledge that
the world is dynamic and diverse.
There is more than just one, there are many.
Each one unique, different and beautiful in its own special
way with equal rights to enjoy from the earth as the other.
A realist will abide by the laws of nature because
he knows whose house he is in and he will live

by his ideals and principles according to his acknowledgement of what is real and around him. You should not be an idealist, but you should be a realist with ideals."

The human mind, and its power, are the most fascinating phenomenon of human existence, I conclude. It powers our existence, perceptions, and perception of being with results as individuals through personality traits, characteristics and idiosyncrasies as there are stars in the Universe. What it is to be human is certainly inextricably linked to the phenomenon of the human mind. Its perceptions through individuals shape our existence. The consequence of all aspects of our existence that is influenced by human beings lies in the phenomenon of the human mind. This is where the power of our freedom lies as our thoughts, ideas and ideals inform action and consequence. The freedom to act that either has positive or negative effects on others and the environment.

To imagine a collective human perspective governed by balanced principles which encapsulate the power of the freedom of the mind against the challenges and realities of existence.

The challenges of reality and how we choose to overcome them through the perceptions of the mind is the source of positive or negative human interaction.

To balance out the reality and practicalities of existence against the reality the mind can create in many variant forms. That is the challenge.

Idealism as a function of the human mind can cause us to develop a reality we want for ourselves defined by any parameters the mind can create. However, what never changes is the reality on the ground.

Having an ideal that espouses racial superiority leads to the inevitable subjugation of other races. Valuing your superiority, dominance, and survival over others and all else, is an ideal that does not fall into balance with the reality on the ground, that others should be valued for the worth of their existence just as equally.

The human mind; what a thing. A universal functional realistic human perspective, what a thing indeed.

2.15 "Be critical of everything you read for it is written by the hand of man.
Never take written print as the ultimate truth. Always search for the truth and always keep your mind awake. Even if it is sacred, the most sacrosanct of parchments, analyse and make your own conclusions. You are your own man, and the master of your own destiny and salvation.
You should never let anyone tell you how to think. Heed their message if it is true, but make that truth your own. Always look for the truth for only each man knows his own true motive.
Therefore, because of this fact, you should be forever vigilant."

The Power of the written word!

The invention of writing set the road toward modern existence. One writes down their ideas and perspectives. Not only can they be reprinted and disseminated in mass to the population, but they can be improved upon if needs be, altered or rearranged. The power of human intelligence combined. However, as ever, by virtue of the Dichotic Dilemma, everything can have a positive or negative effect depending on how it is used or applied.

In the human sphere of existence, we have the phenomenon of religion powered by written words. In the search for God, consequently, we have many texts regarded as the word of God, and the power of the written word is no more evident than within this paradigm with its power to shape human existence and perspective. The influence of modern science is also a factor in this equation as it too has the power to dictate how we live, perceive life, and our beliefs about life.

However, again, it goes back to the power of the written word. It uses the power of a higher authority to dictate human action necessitating social control, which has its positives as it can build cohesion and a moral basis for existence but can also be used to exploit by those wielding that word.

As a victim of colonisation through my racial genealogy, I found it difficult to fathom how these conquerors who subjugated my people were at the same time heralded as messengers of God-spreading civilisation. How could God, benevolent and kind, allow us to be second-class citizens and some even justified this state of existence through words written in the Bible.

The power of the written word breeds the power to control the mind and controlling the mind creates action, and action has consequences. Indeed, human beings need something to believe in to explain our existence and its purpose, and this itself poses another question which is the question of spirituality, the soul or spirit within against the idea of humans just being an evolved highly-complex animal with greater relative intelligence and higher mental function which creates complex emotions, perceptions, and feelings. This is a fundamental life question that I will address further in the book.

However, by virtue of human diversity, so many perspectives exist with their own ideologies and ideas on the same theme, human existence.

The power of the human mind through environmental observation allows us to create these perspectives. However, the fundamental principles of existence remain the same. In the search for a unifying truth, it is looking at these fundamentals always, in the face of diversity that will allow for a realisation of that truth. The realisation of eternal constants is a unifying function.

The power of the written word coupled with the fallibility of human perception means that whatever has been written by the hand of a human being is subject to error and misguidance and we should always be aware of this possibility. Else we will be forever subject to the power of the written word and those who hold it in the human social sphere.

Consequently, when those who say they stand and speak in the name of God holding these holy books exploit, violate and order to kill. Some wonder who or what this God is who allows this to happen. Priests who violate the innocence of little boys, the modern-day televangelists who steal from the poor and fund exceedingly lavish and opulent existences. Death, oppression, and abuse, all in the name of God as people fall prey to the power of the written word and those who wield it. It is to ask what human existence is, what God is that such things can, should, and do happen. What and who are we?

It is by looking at the things that are constant, transcendent, and universal that we can begin to find some answers. The Dichotic Dilemma is the effect of positive and negative, the Universe, the need to survive, our self-awareness, intelligence, and emotional state that allow us to perceive and experience this life.

However, what for?

2.16 "We once all shared the earth, free to
roam and enjoy it as one pleased.
All we ever had to do was respect those who got to
a place first.
But one man came, a greedy, selfish and evil man.
He beguiled the impressionable and unsuspecting.
He killed and subjugated he who was there first.
Raped and pillaged of him his land, women, and children.
He took his loot back to his house.
The "evil" one left the Aboriginals with nothing. Built

large fences and borders around his house so that he could enjoy and feast by himself and only let the other man share after he has begged and pleaded.
The other man cannot fight back because he is wounded, bleeding, and confused by the poison left in him by the one who came as a friend but was the worst of enemies. No, a friend he was not. He was the most vile of villains."

In the transition of time, recent colonial history, as the white race sought to expand its borders and venture into regions unknown in search of wealth and to survive, has created vast imbalances in both the natural world and the human social world of existence, particularly along racial lines. The white race, by and large, enjoyed the fruits of victory and dominion through technological superiority. As a member of a marginalised, defeated, and subjugated group, however, less so in my personal experience but observing from a collective historical point of view, it is easy for me or us to say that white people are evil or bad powered by the perception of difference. However, observing humanity as a singular race, racial them and us is reduced to, us all being a part of the singular human race, which a part of, benefiting from advantage, dominated another and others.

The function of dominion is inter and intra-personal and dictated by the function of natural selection, environmental cues and the survival instinct. Consequently, as the white race spread its borders, many atrocities were committed against the indigenous groups as wars were fought to acquire that dominance. When humanity pushes itself to the extremes of war, dire and regrettable consequences can result as the pressures of functionality reduce the worth of a human being powered by the dictates of the prevailing state of mind. Hence, the result is, we can resort to regrettable methods to win the war, biological warfare being one of the most sinister by virtue of its power, to kill off present and ensuing generations. As was and is the case in many parts of the world that the white race spread to as in the case of the Native Americans by and large. The result of which was the notable depletion of the numbers of Native Americans and the reduction vastly in bison herds as the dictates of a different civilisation were implemented in that region.

However, to speak of evil ones as the poem does is to not reduce or analyse deep enough into the phenomenon as it presented and presents. Questions exist as to how the white race gained the superior technological edge so decisively such that the ensuing warfare was militarily one-sided as the indigenous populations used more basic weaponry. A perspective of different races, which means white people and other races are separate, brings about ideas of racial superiority and such concepts that still exist today in some quarters. However, looking at the human race as a singular means that one can argue that the survival conditions and necessities of one geographical group of the human race meant that, to answer the challenges of survival in that geographical region, the intellectual faculties of human beings allowed for innovations which lead to that technological superiority through the function of time. This perspective allows one to go as far as possible in the timeline of human existence as to even try and understand the very origins of different racial groups. If our humanity is so singular as it clearly is, how do such extreme external variants of the same species exist, ranging from Orientals to Blacks, South Americans, and the many disparate ethnic presentations? Doing so leads to a true understanding and insight into who and what we are as a collective. Many thinkers, past and present, have posed their analytical observations, which are both credible and sound. Just as the Arctic fox is white and its cousins in different climes are brown in colour, we are one with nature. Just as the observation of the skeletal appearance of most animals shows variations on a singular theme as we share the same characteristic skeletal structure, only varying to allow for the diversity of the fauna on the planet.

We are one with nature just as we are a singular group. The human story is one singular story through time. Understanding and appreciating this concept, our interconnectedness and our interconnectedness with the earth and the Universe, a paradigm shift in collective human thinking and perspective, is the key to a more balanced existence.

This is the power of deeper and more intrinsic observation as opposed to falling prey to the superficial observations which blight our understanding of each other and our purpose.

*2.17 "Daily Star: Sunday April 2 2006:- 500 000 refugees
make Easter's number 1 hotspot a HELL HOLE. British
tourists heading for their number 1 holiday hot spot
this Easter will fly into an enormous refugee crisis.
More than 500 000 Africans have targeted
Tenerife as a stepping stone to a new life in
Europe sparking a crisis on the island.
Full story pages 30-31........"
It is a holiday to them, the life of a black man. God,
please make it make sense because I am struggling".*

Social disparity and the struggle to acquire a fair system of resource distribution are encapsulated by the multi-faceted function of being a human being as we look to a God which seems conspicuous only by virtue of its apparent absence.

*2.18 "Being removed from the situation or mentally
standing a bit further back, means I can fully look at
us with no distractions and measure and analyse.
I am drawing comparisons at times and I can see
that none can even begin to compare to you.
You are the highest echelon, a paragon in your own paradigm.
You have your own definition.
You are the epitome, the embodiment of
all that is, what it is to be human.*

*You are beautiful, innocent, and quite simply in
your own class. None can compare.
I end here and I cherish your blessed love. Yes
indeed, beauty still exists on this earth."*

An ode to love. That emotion brings out the beauty in even those things we think are ugly, things we fear, despise and cause us pain and suffering. Love, just a word but in truth and function, is the power of understanding.

*2.19 "Riding in the back seat of my father's car down
this stretch of African road listening to the nostalgic
and rather quintessential sound of Jonas Gwangwa.
Appreciating how it talks to me and tells me a different
story by its different sounds and melodies. What
is that I see through the window as we drive
by?
Two African women silhouetted against
the dusky orange African sky.
Beyond them this panoramic view which
strikes a chord right in my soul.
They have sticks of firewood balanced on their heads
and I can make out that they are engaged in dialogue
as they sway toward an unknown destination.
In a flash, we are past them.
Who were they, what's her name, what were they
talking about?
As we leave them and they fade into the distance, it hits me.
I will never see them again, or here their voices, or share
in their conversation and partake in their laughter.
It is such a beautiful yet joyfully painful, sorrowful
yet nostalgic inexplicable feeling this realisation gives me.*

But what is for certain is that it is such an African experience.
Beauty beyond explanation.
It is so beautiful that I will not spoil this piece
with a lament about the negative.
These women, their lives so simple, so
tranquil, "primitive" even.
They are so insignificant, but are they?
Their lives, I am so confused I fail to conclude. There
is such a truth in their simplicity, an innocence,
some ancient truth I long to understand.
Beauty beyond belief.
But as I come to the end of my ode I realise now that
I am indeed in a foreign land, and reality floods
back to me.
I had my moment."

The manifestation of such disparate, distinct, and different cultures and peoples throughout the globe through the transition of time has made it appear as if we are alien to one another. Our practices, customs, beliefs, even micro and macro geographical variants, create such bridges and gaps that we become so different from one another.

Language barriers, cultural barriers, and such manifestations which create completely disparate perceptions of existence, even more so in areas of vast geographical distance. How can we be one race when we are so different? So dissimilar by virtue of our disparate groups yet so interconnected and intrinsically linked individually and as a collective.

The poem touches on the sheer vastness of the human population. The billions of people you will never meet who seem just as insignificant and distant to you as you are to them in a never-ending seemingly perpetual cycle of human existence. I find the thought staggering. Yet we seem to be dictated upon more by the lesser aspects of existence and fail to realise the majesty of such a perspective in our collective existence as a race.

The beauty of Africa and its people is undeniable as much as the beauty of Asia, Europe, America, the Antarctic and all the peoples of the planet. The eclectic beauty of the planet is ever more emphasised by the diverse presentation of different peoples, just as the natural world is more beautiful by the virtue of diverse flora and fauna. How do we celebrate our individuality and differences cohesively as a whole without allowing these differences to breed tension?

Suffice it to say, when we war and feud, the planet and the cosmos continue to bring forth a new day as silent observers of our fractious existence. It is only ourselves we kill. Time will not stop for us and our planet will continue to be, even if we have exhausted our existence and the resources of this planet through hate and poorly guided ideals. If these nuclear weapons we build as we continue to fear ourselves were to be set upon the earth in war, in a million years, the planet will still be here. Despite us and our absence.

2.20 "You cannot question the unquestionable.
Therefore, you do not question the unquestionable.
For this is the endeavour of naivety.
For all you will find is confusion and ever more questions.
There is NO "TRUTH" or rather, there is no
"TRUTH" to be found, not here, not now.
Everything is relative and circumstantial.
There are no absolutes in life.
There is no absolute truth. Everything is relative.
Stop, else die of a withered spirit and the torture you
will endure from an endless and arduous quest.
Search for the truth and perish, or accept what's in
front of you and make the best of it? That
is the proverbial dilemma.
Accept what is beyond your knowledge and
ability to change or search for the truth and neglect

all that's around you and dear to you?
Is this the price of the truth?
What is the point to life, life as we know it, life as I see it?
I say there is no point, for we are a cursed
species. All we do is curse and destroy.
The truth is there but I have been told it
cannot be found, not here, not now.
I say the point of life for me is NOT to perpetuate
this species for the sooner the earth rids herself of
this "HUMANITY" the better it is for her.
However, the point of life for me is for one to
honour those who have been before you.
Good people like my father and mother who have toiled
and struggled against the odds so I could be here today.
Their endeavour has to be honoured for they
know not why they are here either.
But they are, so I owe it to them and their honour. The point
of my life is to honour them and their effort which has been
great, for this is the only thing that makes sense to me."

There are some things that seem impossible until they are done. To push convention, to challenge an erroneous status quo. Growing up, I internalised human strife so much so that the weight of perceiving only pain and suffering, the negative aspects of existence, was threatening the stability of my own existence. Why was that fundamental question pervading my existence? That is the theme of this poem. The meaning and purpose of existence seemed futile by virtue of my negative perception of the arduous challenges of human existence. However, as ever, I now understand the edifying nature of pain and suffering.

As the poem describes, at that point, I realised the purpose to my existence through my emotional attachments to my family as we all do, in one shape or form, live for our families and loved ones. Perchance however, there is a grander and greater family attachment to be realised. A romanticised ideal indeed for the more pragmatic minds.

However, a noble notion nonetheless, to conclude that a history of infighting to potentially usher in a future of a more balanced existence and coexistence through the understanding acquired from the pain and suffering of that history. The question is how to functionally apply such notions to our human social and collective existence in light of the effect of our lesser nature and lesser selves.

2.21 "The black man's singular and most crucial weakness is his gentle, simple and accommodating nature.
To defeat your foe, you have to know him, and
this is the only way you can counter him.
Else you will open your door, make him a feast never
knowing that you have let in the most villainous of villains.
He will rob you, and you will always fear
him, because you have never known.
He is not great, but you have not known.
So let knowledge REIGN."

Again, the question is, how to functionally let go of the pain of history, the torture, torment, oppression, and killing of others in the name of riches, dominance, superiority, and survival towards a 21st-century existence of enlightened understanding! Let knowledge and understanding reign. A shared knowledge to address the corrupting influence of ignorance.

2.22 "The true sign of the extent of a black man's
oppression is the simple fact that it is seen as the
greatest achievement when one black man manages
to do or achieve what an average white man takes
for granted or can achieve without having to try
much."

The destructive howl of a fractious history will continue to echo into the future in the manifestation of social existence, so again, the challenge is to functionally learn and grow from it. To recognise the human being, the human family. Just as your brother or sister does you wrong, and yet they continue to be your brother or sister even if you only make peace after peace should have been made well before. Your family still remains.

Racial superiority is a nonexistent phenomenon and the apparent presentation of it is only reflective of the recent course of human history which saw racial domination of some racial groups by others. Creating eventual ghettos and the associated subsequent social decay amongst some aspects of the subjugated groups, as would happen in any impoverished social grouping. Within all human beings and racial groups lies the potential for extremes of intelligence and other characteristics and attributes in individuals all along the spectrum by virtue of natural selection. This function naturally creates roles for individuals in society and creates a framework for our existence. It is not a function unique to one group, it is a universal human function and attribute. It is the functional understanding of the concept of the human being, the human family; transcendent and edifying.

2.23 "I am not racist, I reiterate, I am not racist.
At the Olympics, there are many athletes
representing many various types of sports.
If I have come to the Olympics as a 100-metre
sprint runner, when I am consequently
interviewed, I can only speak with full
knowledge on the experience of running a 100-metres.
If one person is standing on platform A, another on
platform B and so on and they can only view the
world from that platform.
They surely can only comment on only the scenery or
scenario they can observe from that vantage point.
Therefore, I am a black man and I see things

from where I stand as a black man.
Thus I can only comment on the truth I
can see from where I can see it.
I, therefore, cannot be racist if I am just
merely Relating the truth I can see.
I am adamantly discriminate towards evil, acts of
evil and in particular the evil acts against those who
look like me because they are me and I am them.
We are brothers of the same struggle and if it wasn't him
it would be me, and if it wasn't me it would be him.
My heart aches as I long to see something
better, a better day and I shall, we all shall for our
spirit is strong."

This piece is a result of self-reflection. I realised that I seemed to be speaking out against people I deemed racist and hated their actions. However, through reading my own words, I realised that potentially I, too, was beginning to sound like a racist. Hence, it becomes a realisation of the effect of action and reaction. If someone shouts abuse at you and you shout back, you can then end up involved in a never- ending spiral of retaliatory action and can then sink to become the lower forms of ourselves that we can be.

Furthermore, at that stage of realisation, it was again, an early appreciation of the effect of perspective and how it poses a lot of moral and social dilemmas and questions. For example, how can you judge someone when in essence, you have never walked in their shoes?

When you fight for your freedom, where is the line whereby the freedom fighter becomes the oppressor and the transgressor? If you say you are here to liberate, how soon do you become a conqueror? The great moral and social dilemmas where perspective becomes the vehicle for legitimised atrocities and wrong and right become the most relative, intangible, and inscrutable of phenomena in our existence. My views were only in retaliation and observation and fully justified by factual observation. However, they were potentially turning me into the thing I despised and proposed to be speaking out against.

That's the power of perspective emphasising ever more so the power of a shared human perspective. The realisation of the human being and the functional and balanced implementation of the ideal globally. It's the only way to end the cycle of hate for the ensuing generations whose challenges to survive will far outstrip ours today in light of increasing human pressure on continually limiting resources. In the realisation that, when the human being is challenged to survive in limited and trying circumstances, civilisation ceases and we become marauders and killers. That is the law of nature and we are challenged to positively counter these limitations.

2.24 "As you grow up, you are made privy to certain truths.
Most significantly, by the context of your circumstances,
the things and people around you. Hence you
"GROW" up and develop around those truths.
However, when you reach man or womanhood, it
is up to you to search for the truth and falsehood in
the truths you have encountered as you grew up.
For this is the only way you can find yourself.
This is the only way to find the person
who hides within yourself.
The person who has been there before you started
learning of the lies and tragedies and
falsehoods which can disconnect you from the truth
and yourself as you go through this life."

Our humanity has been growing up. The evolution of our humanity and consciousness through time and tragedy. Just as a child who is raised by ignorant parents has to learn a better perspective to realise a better world. Our ignorance has blighted us through history and time. We have reached the age of reason today as a child reaches the age of reason as they become an adult, by most accounts, more mature and wise as should be the case. Can our collective consciousness not reach the age of maturity through all the tribulations of its youth?

2.25 *"Heartache, another sure reminder that it is not really as we see it.*
It is not a biological experience, extremely abstract and so unquantifiable by conventional means.
The very experience. It is not as it seems."

2.26 *"I don't hold it against you but I am saying it hurts.*
Misunderstanding, misunderstanding in love.
I do not hold it against you but I am saying it hurts."

2.27 *"The time before the time now, and yes indeed the time after the time now must be a joyous and wonderful time.*
For if it is not, then is anything worth anything?"

2.28 *"What type of person sees another person, recognises a weakness and takes advantage, and discards the other after they have appeased their fickle and very malicious nature? That is the question.*
The most important question is, do they deserve another chance as they recognise the folly in their ways?
Is forgiveness for the foolish, the extremely foolish or is it for the wise, the extremely wise?
The proverbial dichotomy."

2.29 "Is it kindness or foolishness, courtesy before caution?
To see a complete stranger, invite them
into your most sacred place.
The most secret of inner sanctums, your sanctuary.
And then watch them defile, urinate, and defecate on
and all over the things you value the most.
Your honour and dignity.
And still put it past them in the name of all that is Good.
Kindness, love, tolerance, forgiveness.
And let them cause carnage and damage till there
is nothing left of yourself, your most precious
of treasures, nothing left to reclaim.
So who is to blame, the perpetrator or the pacifist? Is it kindness
or foolishness, courtesy before caution? Indeed no good deed goes
unpunished, the Proverbial dichotomy, the proverbial dichotic
dilemma."

The Dichotic Dilemma, the basic instinct, our higher-functioning minds and the presentation of every existential phenomenon with ramifications across the spectrum from positive to negative. The human being is against the factors that input into our existence. We are just but an infinitesimal phenomena in a magnificently and exponentially grand universal space. Who   what are we, wh   our place in this spa ?

CHAPTER THREE!!

Deeper Understanding.
The Road To Enlightenment.

3.1 "There was a truth, a truth that was at the beginning.
This is the truth I seek.
Not the truth as we see it today, but the truth of before.
Alfa.
For if there isn't, then the slightest or most arduous
of endeavours is the paragon of futility."

The age-old question, the most enduring and everlasting of questions, the origin of human beings, the origin of life. To go back far enough in time to see where it all began. Science has its proposals, so does religion, one based on faith and spirituality and the other from observed and calculated analysis and the appreciation of the physical world of material and function. Two sides of the same coin, both interconnected by the phenomenon of existence yet espoused as completely different entities. The Dichotic Dilemma. The question is, how to marry the spiritual with the physical, the supernatural with the factual. The more science discovers the more coincidence and the supernatural are given less credence. The dilemma between religion and science is that a lot of religious texts are still based on the observations of civilisations, very old and past in relation to us in the modern day. Hence, the credibility of some of their assertions have been systematically disproved as the progress of the scientific application of rational thinking has detailed the design of our existence through time. In this way, science plays the role of the heretic and religion, holder and bearer of ancient truths, and the ultimate truth that is God. Hence the assumption that science is Godless and the historical discordance between the two. I argue that the two are indivisible as they are the result of, pervaded, and permeated by the phenomenon of the human being.

However, as the poem purports, to be able to go back in time right to the beginning, if there is such a thing, is to observe the disrobing of all the mystery and wonder of our existence and Universe. In the 21st century, science finds itself close to that point if so as the protagonists of that form of thinking try and unlock the properties of subatomic structures and particles which hold understanding as to the constituents of matter and such theoretical paradigms. In essence, attempting to find out what makes up the Universe. With the baseline argument of detailed scientific discovery as to the origins of the Universe being the Big Bang theory.

I am not a particle physicist or hold such advanced scientific knowledge but my line of argument is based on making what I believe to be simple but incontestable assertions based on reductionist deduction. Hence, on that basis, I refute the idea of the Big Bang as I believe it to be a fatally flawed assumption. I do not refute, however, the obvious genius of the human beings who have made discoveries to this point of deduction at the expense of concluding in some cases that there is no God. In my view again, it becomes the manifestation of the Dichotic Dilemma and the fallibility of human beings. To be so incredibly gifted and intelligent as to be able to calculate and understand such profound ideas and phenomena, yet miss the point by the virtue of becoming blinkered in a perspective. Hence on this basis, I propose a perspective on God which is both scientific and spiritual and bridges the gap between these two constructs and also hopefully goes a way to explaining human existential dilemma in relation to the existence of God.

All human beings on this planet are human beings. Scientists, religious men and women, those classed thieves, murderers, teachers, doctors, lawyers, blacks, whites, Iranians, Turks, Zimbabweans, FreeMasons, Illuminati and so on and so forth, in this plane, all human beings. We know that we have been in this plane of existence credibly from when writing began and the documentation of our existence began. Hence, before that, we know nothing conclusively and that is why the knowledge of our origins as a species here is irrevocably unknown to us and ambiguous to our understanding. There is no documentation right at the point of our creation but incontestably, we have to have come from somewhere.

Hence, if our state of consciousness was our initial starting point of self awareness as human beings, with no other evidence of our origin, it seems the first natural thing to do is to look for our creator, our origins. Consequently, the first tangible construct to our existence becomes the idea of God or a creator.

Human spread is evident through our proliferation and presence in different parts of the earth as we present as different racial groups, characteristics that have brought about different theoretical schools of thought as to how the different racial groups were formed. An argument proposed, for example, is that there was a potential point source, which was the cradle of civilisation through evolutionary process when the earth was once a single body called Pangea. Where from, the resultant spread of life to different parts of Pangea subsequently made permanent by tectonic drift resulted in different- looking strands of the same creatures by virtue of environmental adaptation. A credible idea that is at odds with religious doctrines such as Christianity as it is one of the more dominant religions through conquest which dictates that God is the creator of all and "He" made us and the Universe as the story of Genesis implies. This is an idea that has created a humanistic God with anger and other attributes who capriciously intervenes and intercedes in human existence for His so- called Chosen Ones. Thus, creating into the 21st century a debate and friction between those who factually seek to understand our existence and those who espouse this God.

Distorting and creating intellectual divisions and rifts inter- and intra-personally between the pursuit of the factual understanding of human existence and the didactic approach of the Bible and more espoused ancient books. Some which in part decry the questioning nature and unfortunately reflect in some ways the views of societies far passed who held beliefs that do not reflect the mental state of a 21st century technological world.

How these ancient texts were compiled and happen to dominate humanity in many parts of the world is an erudite matter for historians and theologians. However, mine is not to refute their entire validity but to bridge a gap between all schools of thought that seem divided but are essentially a reflection of a singular humanity.

The point to be made is that the potency of the Bible in many ways as a dominant perspective was facilitated by imperialist dictates, consequently nullifying the input of the perspectives of the dominated groups. Creating a human-prescribed idea of God, the God who intervenes in our lives, hence why people ask, "Why then do bad things happen if God supposedly loves us so much? Where is God when there is killing and brutality? Essentially, why does God allow bad things to happen?"

So who and what is God?

The question is, if there is only one God, then how come different religions and groups of people speak of different Gods and that their God is the only true God? Again, it is to go back to the argument of evolutionary human spread and our first port of call as we cower to the burdens of human existence and the need to survive by crying out to higher powers for help. Through time, different civilisations adopted different ways of doing this through their environmental cues. Some worshipped nature and respected it as they sensed the symbiosis between us and it and how we are reliant on nature ultimately for our survival. This is characterised in different cultures and in different ways as many ancient cultures spoke of water Gods, animal Gods, sun Gods, rain Gods and such as they appreciated how their survival was intrinsically linked to these phenomena. However, to look up and seek God or supernatural intervention is our first port of call when we cannot fully dictate the result of our own survival. This idea helps explain the proliferation of seemingly many Gods and is quite simply the result of different cultures, groups, and peoples doing the same thing but applying nuanced names, customs, and traditions based on their knowledge base, perspective, and environmental interaction.

The idea of the superiority of just one God lends itself more to imperialist pursuits and spread which consequently also meant and means doctrinal spread on the basis that controlling the mind is controlling the masses and the masses of the conquered groups. It is a human contrived mechanism exploiting the dictates of our basic function to look for God as we seek to understand ourselves but being used as a mechanism to install power dominance and control over a conquered group.

The widely-held belief of the Judeo-Christian, Islamic God who loves and cares for us in a humanistic way and has transmitted his word directly into the books of the faiths has created confusion in our consciousness as we face the dictates of our lesser selves and the challenges of existence. War, hate, racism, death, famine, wealth divide, general human malaise, suffering, and disease. If God loves us, where is "He"?

Furthermore, those who believe in supernatural intervention look for God in things they call miracles. A supposedly extra-ordinary twist of fate as God saves His children. For example, the Chilean miners who survived in the collapsed mine as was televised worldwide in the year 2010 in some quarters was seen as an act of God. However, analytical and questioning minds quickly point to the proliferation of suffering in spite of this supposed intervention and point to factual observations which explain the so-called miracle. Hence, on this basis, a truly fair God does not intervene in human existence because its very intervention in one person's existence is at the expense of another, immediately creating a state of unfairness and imbalance. Consequently, I deduce and conclude that God does not play a part in human existence, however, that is not to say God does not exist. The mandate is on us to create a fair and balanced existence for ourselves by understanding and implementing the higher values which create harmony and balance. The educational process is our responsibility because, how do we learn otherwise? Consequently, the crux of the issue is the definition of God.

As a young Christian growing up, I was taught to believe that we suffer because we do not understand the will of God and that "He" works in mysterious ways. However, defined as a loving God, allowing some to exploit, kill, and abuse others or little children to be raped and killed, the existence of child soldiers, and other expressions of negativity in our existence seems not mysterious but cruel. However, this is blamed on the devil. This idea however, is even more irrational and creates terrifying constructs in the human mind of demons, evil, and hell. This confounds understanding as others are branded good or evil in the most extreme, unbalanced and non-analytical ways which create an ominous perception of human existence, perpetuating the idea of human suffering as being the work of the devil. This idea in my view is barbaric, outdated, dysfunctional, and disempowering to the power of a universal understanding which will highlight that under the right conditions and perspective, we have the power to facilitate a better existence for ourselves. It is an irrational ideal and idea. Laying the responsibility onto the devil or God justifies some behaviours because the conclusion is that those people are bad and it perpetually separates us. Whereas, an analytical and balanced assessment looks into the contributory elements to that behaviour and concludes that, if those are availed, those behaviours would most possibly not occur. Do we wait for God to help us and blame the devil for mal-consequence or do we acknowledge that, we live here in a physical plane and acknowledge that our actions and the consequence of physical forces affect outcomes? Respecting and understanding nature, our own nature and the need for balance.

The proposal is that God exists but not necessarily in the way defined by the present dominant human religions which turn human beings into good and evil people, the redeemed and infidels, God's Chosen

Ones and the rest being savage dogs. They are divisive constructs which underline our lesser functions and pervading effect of the survival instinct to survive through dominance. Hence, God exists but what is confounding our understanding is our definition of God. To observe just the phenomenon of existence from any perspective and position irrevocably alludes to the existence of a supernatural being, presence or force beyond our understanding.

Scientists are not a breed apart, they are not evil people trying to end the world. They are human beings who seek understanding, analysts trying to find out how and why we are, that elusive panacea. Human beings who, by all accounts, are just like every other human being, find themselves in a certain role at a certain time, fulfilling a particular destiny brought about by factors intrinsic and extrinsic. Functionally, they are rational minds and in the simplest terms, science is the implementation of structured, analytical, investigated, and detailed common sense. Anyone who rationalises or seeks understanding that is not confounded by ignorance is a scientist. As human beings, we get caught up in terminology and wide-ranging sweeping generalisations which create constructs and caricatures of situations and other human beings confounding the universal realisation that they are still just but human beings. Hence, by virtue of everything presenting on the spectrum from one extreme to another, some "scientific" or analytical minds are gifted with the power of understanding which leads to greater more intrinsic observations through the bodies of learning now established, normalised and made systemic and systematic in the 21st century. However, they are still simple human beings confined in this existential space we call earth.

Some will believe in the Christian and monotheistic God, and some will not, and some will hold other beliefs as reflective of the cross section of all human beings on the planet. That is the function of being human beings. Science is not a phenomenon outside humanity, it is an extension of it, and espousing its function is not ungodly. Questioning is a route to understanding and not questioning is the route to ignorance.

As ever, the dilemma is how to do so whilst best preserving the principles of respecting human life and all life. Hence, I view "scientific" understanding as an effort to try and understand "God" in a practical and physical way and understanding God leads to higher enlightenment. However, that method of trying to understand God should not be seen as separate from the dilemma of human existence. Equally so, looking for God through human beings and life in a spiritual way is just as important. Understanding God through observing ourselves socially, who and what we are also leads to higher enlightenment. The two pursuits are not and should not be divisive, they should be indivisible and a reflection of the Dichotic Dilemma. In essence, two extremes of perception coming together for the betterment of all human beings.

All religions in their core beliefs speak about existential cohesive understanding and co-existence of all human beings. The confounding variable has been the need to survive which pits us directly against each other and becomes the conduit towards human abuse of one another and the natural environment. The voyage of scientific discovery has abated the constraints of human survival through the invention of technology. Hence, the aggregation of the two constructs, spirituality through the positive teaching of long held knowledge and beliefs and the advance of technology to ease survival conditions, should result in a higher understanding of our purpose and facilitate co-existence. A multi-perspective aggregation of all past and present human knowledge as all faiths and perspectives have valuable knowledge to offer.

What is God in the light of such a perspective? God becomes totality, everything, the understanding and cohesion of all the input aspects of existence. God becomes the Universe and we are an extension of that universal body existent on this earth in a physical plane trying to understand our interconnectedness to this seemingly elusive entity.

How is God the Universe? If understanding the elemental aspects of the Universe is learning God's mind as Einstein once said, understanding the process of creation and existence, then God and the Universe become indivisible. Understanding nature and the Universe is understanding the building blocks of the creator and the creator itself.

Consequently, where does the Big Bang theory of creation fit into this perspective? It becomes a very erudite perspective reflecting the power and the marvel of the human mind but remains still but that, a product of human observation. Our powers are limited by our fallibility.

Evolution and all other perspectives of trying to understand and explain life, creation and our origins become a conduit towards the how, as ever, the why being the elusive construct.

I argue that you cannot have something out of nothing. You cannot create into a space where there was no space before. Hence, the existence of life and us in it means something has always existed to facilitate this existence. The logical question becomes, how can something always be? An idea that confounds human understanding. The idea of perpetuity, time not having a starting point. The physical idea that begins to paint a more majestic idea of God than the capricious and punitive God who at times seems egomaniacal and vengeful as "He" punishes us to test our loyalty and servitude to "Him". An irrational construct of God born through emotional human perception during the grip of trying times.

Hence God is fair by leaving us to fend for our own destiny positively by realising the importance of understanding and balance: universal understanding and balance through lessons learnt through time. Again, pain is a teacher, and I propose that, that is the mystery of God's ways. Pain is only alleviated when understanding is gained and balance is created. God is the Universe which exists by the virtue of the balance of opposing forces. To become more like God, we have to understand the concept of balance. In this life, yes it is an efficacious theoretical perspective. A theoretical perspective that espouses interconnectedness and oneness between the human element of existence, its surroundings and phenomena beyond its plane of dominance. The question, however, is whether or not this knowledge is transferred into another life after death in the form of a transcendent spiritual being for existence in some form of higher plane or is it just a lesson for humanity to learn for use in this plane of existence?!

We cannot just be a being of flesh when you consider the complexity of human existence and the complexity of a human being and the human mind. Where is the physical and spiritual contact point within the human body, the link between the body and the soul if such a thing is? Maybe it's a link so intrinsic, subtle, and impossible to detect that it speaks to the power of the unity of intrinsically linking perceived opposites in the pursuit of a higher and enlightened understanding! As the last sentence in the piece says, "For if there isn't, then the slightest or most arduous of endeavours is the paragon of futility." Meaning that, in light of the grandeur and the phenomenal feat of human existence in all its tribulations, there has to be something more to it and to come out of it, otherwise, any effort in the grander scheme of things seems futile and inconsequential as we, at times, struggle with this existence and understanding it.

What are we, flesh or spirit? Transcendent or just beings to live once and die? A soul or just an advanced ape and primate? The aggregation of different seemingly polar and disparate perspectives in the realisation that a singular perspective is always limited, but a universal perspective is indeed, universally binding, edifying and enlightening. Eclecticism as a principle and an existential ideal, UNIVERSAL.

3.2 "A mistake is an action carried out unknowing of the consequence.
For if you had known the outcome, only a
fool would carry out the action.
Therefore, do not live in the past, but learn from it. Live in the present and let the past be the guide into your future.
For we do not have foresight, but we have hindsight
which can help assisting with forecasting the
events that might lie ahead of our actions."

Echoing the aforementioned sentiments, learning from and through pain, I believe in listening to and trying to learn from each and every perspective that human beings possess. The most fascinating thing I have found when looking into the existential perspectives of different schools of thought is how in their own right, they are sound and valid by the investigation into the ideas they teach and their factual proof towards that end. Even more so, is how many perspectives there are as to our origins, some which measured against conventional and mainstream schools of thought, seem outlandish. For example, some schools of thought suggest our ancestry being linked to "aliens".

However, as ever, the crux of the matter becomes, how do we define what an alien is? The spoofing and caricaturing of the idea of extraterrestrials has taken away from the valid reference to such an idea in the mainstream. However, if there is an afterlife or ascension into some other plane, such an existence is an "extra-terrestrial" phenomenon. Furthermore, some schools of thought propose that our technological leaps are related to the influence of extraterrestrials. Are we alone as that famous phrase enquiries? Again, who and what are we? In my search for understanding of our existence, I do not discount any perspective, however, I just interrogate its validity and how it relates to our physical existence here on this planet and our strife by all accounts.

For example, Hindu faith teaches reincarnation. In the context of human existence when you look at the actions of people termed bad, for example, the brutal dictators and oppressive people that we have all around us in day to day life, the question is, do they face a sentence for their actions? Parallel against the deterministic functions that dictate our actions and outcomes. Hence, in the context of reincarnation, in the search for social justice, it seems valid to propose that they come back to maybe learn against that negative energy which they would have exhibited through their existence. That is to say if we are a spiritual being or a soul as it were.

The difficulty with the idea of a soul inhabiting the body as a host, so- to-speak, is created by observing the physical brain and learning how the different chemicals or even altering the physical constituents of it can seemingly change who a person is or their characteristics and demeanour. Cartesian dualism, where do you draw the line? As the school of science delves further into the body and investigates the machine and hardwiring that is the physical human body, the apparent mystery of existence and how we experience life is dispelled as emotions become just neurological inputs and dictates of how we feel and act become functions stored, controlled, and propagated by different parts of the brain. However, by any definition, ultimately, it's undeniable to conclude that there is an element to life undoubtedly that feels metaphysical and alludes to a spiritual feeling and sense. That churning of emotions that is both intangible and seemingly just outside the bounds of the physical state and thus determining how we perceive life.

However, maybe the host and the body are one and so interlinked in this plane such that you cannot have one without the other and the crucial realisation is that as long as we are here, the physical input is the most determining as it dictates how life is experienced. Learning from everyone and understanding the role of everyone and everything creates the bigger and more holistic picture. Eclecticism.

3.3 "In a relationship, no one has the right to stop someone from living their life.
To stop them from fulfilling themselves as a human being.
To stop them from finding who they are in the journey of life.
However, in a relationship you owe each other
respect, respect when you are in each other's
presence and respect when you are apart.
Thus in this way you can help not hinder each other's
growth as you try to find and fulfil your purpose."

Existence is a relationship of all the interrelated parts. That relationship can either be positive or negative by the virtue of the actions of those constituent parts. It is the obligation of the partners involved in a relationship, therefore, to ensure that the outcome of the relationship is positive.

3.4 *"A great knowledge has been lost in the transition of time and it is my greatest wish to realise the truth before I am fully consumed by this confusion around me. I do NOT want to lose track, I want the truth."*

Clearly, from the observation of this piece, I was and always have been intrigued by finding out the deeper meaning of life as I am sure most people are. This piece was to say, I was aware of the potentially corrupting influence of life as I got older and did not want to be "consumed" by the confusion of life as I would be forced to be an active part of it as an adult. However, now I believe that nothing is ultimately corrupting as long as you learn from it and abide by and advance that newfound knowledge. Each occurrence is an opportunity to observe and learn from the different aspects of life, both positive and negative in search of greater and grander realisations.

A great knowledge has been lost in time! I am fascinated by the history and knowledge base of great and ancient civilisations. Most notably in the mainstream, civilisations such as the Mayans, Inca, Aztecs, Sumerians and ancient Egyptians. There are many other ancient civilisations less known that existed through time periods and had perceptions, technology, and understanding that still baffles us today as to how they managed to achieve what they did from the basic tools they are proposed to have had. In my own country of origin stands what is called the Great Zimbabwe Ruins. These are structures made of stone cut and moulded to such precision that they still stand today even after centuries without mortar or cement to bind the structures together. Kingdoms built into the mountains with passageways that defy the perceived technological capabilities of the people at the time.

In the context of living in London England in the 21st century as a young African black male human being, one realises that, in the transition of time, so much has happened. It inculcates even more so the sense of trying to link with this history, all these people, times and periods of human existence with a 21st-century life that seems so far away and alien from these perspectives. All in an effort to understand the past and those human beings in the context of their relationship to the human beings today; an understanding towards enlightenment for the future to come.

3.5 "Modern living is just a big distraction from ultimate truth that a very malevolent force will not allow us to find out."

It is to wonder whether or not the functional day-to-day existence of life experienced in any time period produced a different tangibility to human existence. Going through life on a day-to-day basis and going to our jobs, some seemingly banal and bland, can create mundanity to existence which in turn can create a spiritual void. Spirituality being the phenomenon which gives life that fulfilling quality and feel to it; that intangible upliftedness.

I wrote this piece when I lived in inner-city London, the concrete jungle characterised to some extent by the constricting feel of perceived deprivation. The feeling produced was as such expressed in the piece when one can feel and question, "is there more to life?", particularly in the context of my surroundings at the time in a modern inner city. Little wonder why these places are characterised by crime and the lesser aspects of human existence as humanity is "locked up" in deprived concrete tower blocks with no aspirations and subject to a limited perspective. A sad indictment to modernity. A modernity which could achieve so much for humanity in relation to its greater achievements.

3.6 "We mask our greatest fears behind a frown, an angry face, a punch.

"The greatest form of defence is attack", and we are civilised?
No, the greatest form of defence is getting in touch with the problem, rooting it out, and essentially getting to know yourself.
Then you are invulnerable, you have no weakness.
For your strength comes from within.
They might break the outside, for your outside is vulnerable, but the barrier they find inside will be impervious to anything they can throw at you.
Thus a frown is just a shield, a penetrable shield, but the force of a smile is even, ever more powerful.
There is a deep, powerful and complex truth to be found there."

I will let this one speak for itself.

3.7 "You should never, I repeat never, put all your trust in a person for that is utter foolishness.
You should put all your trust in yourself because only you have ultimate control over your own actions and if you trust yourself, you can trust that you have put your faith in the right person.
Never put all your trust in another person,
for they are just but a person.
For they might mean well and never have any intention to do you wrong if you are lucky.
But they still are just a person, and sometimes we know not the consequence of our own actions.
Sometimes we lose control and in many
cases we just do not have control.
Trust only yourself, others, be shrewd and only a few others, let them in as they prove themselves, but only so far!!!!

*In doing so, you reserve some strength for yourself
so that if they were to betray you, at least you still
have some strength to be able to recover.
Else they will take everything you have and your
soul and you will be left empty, cold and bitter.
Just but a meagre shadow of yourself."*

We are all human beings on this planet and that should be the basis of our interaction always. Respect, freedom of speech, fairness, and equality. Equality being the realisation that, to allow for the function of existence, hierarchy is important. Hence, as such, some will be at the top and some at the bottom to fulfil cohesive existential function.

However, equality dictates that those who are at the top should respect those at the bottom in equal measure. Respect them for their worth as human beings because you cannot have one without the other. Top needs bottom and bottom needs top, each important in their own right, function, and ultimately, human value. Understanding this is understanding God, understanding balance. No light without dark, positive without negative. Each plays a part in completing the whole and creating balance and life. In the human social sphere, this notion equates to respect, respect for each human being. Fairness and equality. Equality in the value of function, equality in human worth. Else we will forever bemoan an imperfect and unfair world when it is not the world and the Universe who are imperfect, but us.

No one dictates ultimately and outright the conditions of their existence. It is always the confluence of factors mitigated upon by things that are beyond our control. Respecting these facts is a way towards respecting ourselves and others. To understand the beauty and see the beauty of perceived imperfection is to understand God.

3.7 *"Love is a very powerful force, capable of destroying everything in its path if it's not contained.*

*Therefore, you need to realise it, harness it and then
once it is in your control you can watch it flourish in
you and in everything around you into the
most beautiful of beautiful rose gardens.
For this is real love.
It is your obligation to control and understand it for this world
is like a garden full of thorns and vultures waiting to hinder
love every time it tries to rise from the ground and show itself.
Therefore, protect it as it grows and help it avoid
the thorns so it can grow into the finest, most
robust of trees and watch it as it shelters all*

Balance, the un rstanding of God, the understanding of the Universe.

CHAPTER FOUR!!

"There are absolutes in this world, but what is not absolute is human knowledge, understanding and experience by the virtue of subjective knowledge, understanding and experience."

The birth of "ECLECTICISM"

"ECLECTICISM" realised

4.1 "The truth is circular, for that is
how you complete the cycle.
It has to be explicable within itself and that is why
it needs to entail all knowledge for it has to be
omniscient in its very nature for it to be the truth.
It has to be able to account for any possible eventualities and
be unfalsifiable for it is the truth, and that is common sense.
"ECLECTICISM".

The things that divide us are myriad and vast. Creating seemingly completely different human beings with different outlooks and perspectives. We are different interpersonally and intrapersonally. Wars and negative acts are conducted on the basis of a discerned difference. Psychologists have demonstrated through studies and research how easy it is to create fault lines between humanity by assigning them to different groups. As soon as a division is formed, great or small, animosity can easily follow and this phenomenon transcends all groups and peoples. Them and us, strength in numbers, pack and mob psychology, the basic survival instinct. Like animals we are, on the basis of this observation. Just like packs of wolves, we identify with groups, both natural and manmade in order to draw strength from the safety of our group. Race, fraternities, so-called secret societies, tribal, religious and many other groupings. Eclecticism means you always consider the other person's perspective and position.

My observation is that if there is a truth, the truth then, by its very nature, never changes. Consequently, there cannot be a better truth or a more powerful truth or a truth overriding all truths, there can only be that one truth. Different religious teachings and groups, philosophical and political points of view teach and maintain that their position is right and is the truth. Allah is the only true God. Jehovah is the only true God; Buddha, Vishnu, and many other names given to Gods or God depending whether it's a mono or polytheistic belief system. Only through Jesus Christ can you get to heaven, you need to be baptised and have a certificate to authenticate this initiation. The many ritualistic practices of different faiths that grant one access to be part of and benefit from being in that group. I wonder if this is a heavenly criteria or an earthly criteria to allow for one's acceptance into a group separate from others? Hence, why I believe in humanity as one and believe in action, physical action, against others whether positive or negative as the simple parameter to be the basis of judgement over someone's positive worth.

Communism is wrong. Socialism is wrong. Capitalism is wrong. Individualism versus Collectivism. Creationism versus Evolution. Functionalism versus Spirituality. Money. If all is wrong, then what is right and where is the missing link? Eclecticism argues that none are wrong. The weakness is in our inability to make the systems work fairly and that the missing link is found where we fail to consider fairly and in a balanced way the points, positive points of each contributing perspective to create a better understanding.

If there is only one God, then the missing link is the phenomena of having different perspectives. Eclecticism argues that we all see the same thing but give it different definitions from our different points of origin and understanding. Hence, understanding and realising that singular truth is a process of understanding and learning from those different perspectives. Yet, we stay entrenched in our positions, that survival instinct, the fear of losing one's ascendency. However, fear is a negative emotion which creates paranoia and limits objective judgement and positive actions thus limiting understanding. Eclecticism argues that we are all one, everything is interconnected, so there is nothing to fear but everything to understand.

The truth is circular, a perfect shape. A singular closed smooth unit and system where from its centre, all points are equidistant and equal just as the different perspectives should give each other equal credence to complete the full circle of understanding. The over implementation and domination of one opinion disrupts the smooth outline of the circle, the smooth outline of the truth causing disruption, instability, and inequality. By the virtue of different points of origin or different perspectives, one cannot deny the truth that someone else sees because each has seen from their position and perspective. However, instead of fighting by virtue of a lack of identical understanding, learning from one another so as to benefit from the position and perspective of others and create a more accurate and balanced appreciation is the function of Eclecticism. Hence, we avoid becoming subject to observing the same thing but from different individual vantages then consequently missing the bigger and fuller picture. To argue superiority is to create imbalance, to embrace an Eclectic perspective is to learn from, appreciate, and understand others and the "truth" they see in the hope of realising a greater, better, yet ultimate constant and singular, truth.

Eclecticism, the function of respect and understanding.

4.2 "Change is an intrinsic facet to existence,
a fundamental, universal law.
The world is dynamic, nothing is stagnant,
if so only for a numerical period.
Therefore, what is today is most likely not going to be
tomorrow and probably was not an aeon ago.
It is this principle that dictates that we have to keep
an open mind and always be prepared and
anticipate for the eventuality of change.
Therefore, you should not fear change but embrace it and try
to understand it for it has not occurred for no reason at all.
Some things change, and some are constant.
The constant and the changing, in equal
measure should create a balance.
The constant will help you understand the non-constant."

Change. The force of powers beyond our control. Some despise change as it brings new challenges and interrupts the established ideals of what they hold true and value in that period of time. However, change can either be for the better or the worse, the Dichotic Dilemma. I believe in positivity and on that basis, adapting positively to the eventualities of change. I once hated my colonial history and hated the perceived change and effect I initially concluded it had had on the state of the people and the country I originally only identified with. However, adaptation is the key to survival, even more so positive adaptation to the dictates of new surroundings. Human adaptation is a process of learning and understanding. Therefore, my understanding of the mechanisms which brought about that change have allowed me to turn that hate into a more positive perspective by understanding the dynamism of our existence which means change is constant. Forces exist outside of us which can completely come and upset the parameters of your existence as the colonists did to the indigenous populations of my land of origin. Hence, one should be forever ready for and positively anticipate the eventuality of change. It is part of life in a grander space.

Just as we live, age, and die, and we must, that change is necessary to allow for birth and rebirth. Death is a part of life, our challenge is to make sure it comes under balanced conditions which allow for positive adaptation and understanding. Without death, there is no chance for new life. A fulfilled existence means one does not fear death because they would have understood life.

Equally so, as a humanity we need to adapt to the dictates of our new surroundings if we are going to survive the effects of a new world we have created unwittingly or otherwise.

Where we once fought with spears, bows and arrows and swords, we now fight with advanced weaponry which means one man or woman in a jet or other form of mechanised weaponry, can lay waste to a whole nation. If ever there was a time to positively embrace change, in the name of the realisation of a singular humanity, it is now. Holding onto the old ideals of difference can wreak unpalatable devastation.

Eclecticism, the mindset of a 21st-century world. What the mind sees, we take action. If our minds see unity, we will be united. If our minds functionally understand the efficacy of a singular humanity, we will live in that world.

4.3 "We know everything of their "his-story" and nothing of our "his-story" apart from the fact that we were slaves and any positive black person who has risen to significantly stand for black interests has been summarily silenced and eliminated. Most notably, Malcolm X, Martin Luther
King, and Marcus Garvey.
No wonder we are so defeated and confused, we have no idea of who we are and where we have come from."

The writings of a young mind seeing only a narrow and singular perspective. Such thoughts lived in me, hatred, vengeance, indignation and anger. Who is to imagine what thoughts lived inside the minds of Hitler, Idi Amin Dada and many like them and myself who burnt and burn with a sense of indignation and contempt for others and the potential worlds they create, created and will create through narrow-minded perceptions. Yet I realised how limited my scope was from the benefit of living in a place like London. A place where a myriad of races and cultures are forced to interact through living in a confined space. I realised the humanity, the intrinsic similarity of the many people I interacted with beyond the caricatures and stereotypes. That common thread when all else is stripped away where you connect as just beings, that common thread that speaks of the humanity we all share, the simple goals we desire. Those moments of togetherness we should harness and live by, but seldom do and at most times, only for a flicker. Such as when in war, both sides call a ceasefire and the opposing soldiers meet in no man's land and play a game of football as recorded in wars gone by. Those moments when you save the life of your enemy. The moments of clarity where we realise the folly of our ways only to regrettably carry on when our differing ambitions come crushing back in.

Hence, my views were challenged through introspection and I realised the potentially devastating effect of narrow-minded perceptions as we see every day in our personal lives and in the wider range of our universal social sphere of existence. The effects of an inward need for self preservation prohibiting the realisation of greater things far beyond the self. Greater realisations of a singular humanity, a Universe, an Eclectic realisation and understanding of all things that make, and are, our life and human existence.

Eclecticism, a broader scope.

4.4 "People are quick to judge, quick to highlight the faults in others and hence conceal to themselves and others the faults within themselves.

No one can judge another for no one is without fault.
Be yourself and everything else will come to pass.
A judgement awaits, I hope......"

All the mass murders, killing, genocides, hate, and wars are done and have been done on the basis of an assessment that the group at the other end of the gun are bad, evil, less than worthy, immoral, or subhuman. An automatic assumption that the people and views on your side are good, righteous, worthy, moral and reflective of greater human beings. At least that is the observation on the surface. A more intrinsic assessment analyses the functional inputs that lead to these erroneous assessments. Ill advised doctrines, perceived differences, conformity, instinct, the more deterministic influences of nature and nurture that inform our actions on a day-to-day basis in ways that can be very far away from our conscious observations as we go by our day- to-day lives. Consequently, we then fall prey to them and wreak havoc on us all, and at most times without even realising it. Eclecticism means understanding, appreciating, and incorporating myriad human perspectives, equally respecting the views of others, observing and tolerating with respect their merits and perceived flaws as we all have merits and flaws, each and every one of us. The contrary being as the piece suggests in its closing statement, will be forever ruing the state of our existence hoping and pleading that one day those we perceive to be transgressors will be judged by forces with greater powers than our own which can bring parity and balance to perceived imbalances till the infinite depths of future and time.

Eclecticism is the appreciation of the totality of a human being, the totality of the human race, the totality of the Universe, and the intrinsically interconnected state of all aspects of it. Eclecticism is the appreciation of the necessity of light and darkness, positive and negative, seemingly disparate entities and perspectives, a fundame al symbiosis appr iated only by intrinsic Eclectic, balanced understanding and observation.

Chapter Five!!

The "DICHOTIC DILEMMA" realised

At this stage I am having to remind myself the purpose of this book, this process, and why I am writing. This is brought about by my difficulty at times with coming to terms with some of the ideas I expressed earlier in my life when I wrote them. I find that some embarrass me, some seem neurotic, some seem controversial and uncomfortable to discuss and some seem underdeveloped. Hence, I am having to remind myself at this stage, why I am undertaking this process.

I am doing this to engage with the young man I was when I initially wrote this book. To engage with the human being I was then, his feelings and thoughts which lead to the perceptions he made. A young man who was not my invention but an invention of the world he lives and lived in, a world that frustrated him and the resultant perceptions he developed. I am realising that to have a greater understanding of myself and my necessity, I have to finish this process and confront all my earlier thoughts however they present. They are a reflection of my subconscious, my subconscious motivations, my thoughts which would have informed how I would have lived out my life had I not confronted them. I have to understand the source of all my anger and my prejudices as they are attributes I developed from being exposed to human existence in the way I uniquely was, as we all are. I must try to understand life, my existence, and necessity by understanding myself, my thoughts and putting them into a functional framework that allows me to make sense of my existence and hopefully impart a positive perspective with regards to our existence.

I can say with measured confidence that the more I write, the more my writing is shaping my perspective as through my writing, I am realising a different perspective. A perspective I believe is a positive perspective in light of the more limiting and frustrating aspects of our existence. By doing so, the aim is to address the necessity of a world and existence that at one point and I am sure at many other points in people's lives seems futile and draining. So I will again restate the perspective and framework I use to extrapolate from existence.

I believe in the Dichotic Dilemma as the baseline observation. How everything is either positive or negative and every interaction is measurable on this basis by virtue of its resultant effect on an outcome. Everything revolves around this relationship in varying degrees of extremes. Extremes being the second observation that the extent of extremity, the positivity or negativity of the phenomenon denotes how much effect it has with regards to its disruption of a balanced state.

As human beings on this planet in our current state, our most distinguishing attribute is our comparatively higher cognitive mental capabilities in relation to other animate creatures existing alongside us on this planet. This also forms a tenet for my extrapolation allied against our basic instincts, our lesser selves, the more primal aspects of ourselves which, too, affect our existence. Fundamentally, the survival instinct alongside the sexual instinct creates urges which manifest into our social existence as perceived vices depending on the moral framework we use and the extremes they can lead us to. Greed, selfishness, rape, murder, the urges to be superior, oppressive, and dominant. Racism, tribalism, egotism, and other lesser human attributes prevent a balanced and harmonious existence.

The whole undertaking, a process of reductionist observation on the basis that unveiling and going through the layers of what it is to be a human being will hopefully remove to some degree the veil of confusion and misunderstanding which leads to anguish and pain through our actions. An effort to show that, in this plane of existence, the only thing we have to fear and fight against is ourselves. There are no phantoms, demons and monsters that will harm us except those we create ourselves. We must unveil the deterministic forces which power our behaviour so that at that point we can indeed exercise our freewill through our actions, its freewill powered by a positive perspective.

I believe that if you trace back every human being to their point of delivery into this plane of existence and the resultant input they receive from their existence whilst factoring in their innate attributes, you can explain and understand their human behaviour. So that a rapist is not evil but a result of certain deterministic factors which if mitigated against, through a positive existence, on most accounts, that behaviour will not be exhibited. What goes in, most invariably comes out, the input and output system of us human beings in our social existence.

Child soldiers are not murderers but they indeed certainly become that by observing the environment around their existence. We learn our traits and in adulthood we live them consequently charting human existence and our emotions then colour that existence. I believe that emotional turmoil is a result of a lack of balanced understanding. If you understand your emotional pain and its cause, then it is alleviated. Balance.

Ultimately leading to that final question, what happens after death? Is there an afterlife? Certainly our actions affect the consequence of the afterlife, metaphysical or not. Our actions affect the future life after we have passed. Hence, my position is that, whilst on this earth, we have to prepare for the afterlife, most importantly, the physical afterlife for those that remain after us in our place. Invariably, we live on after our death through those that come after us. The afterlife beyond is a matter for that realm of existence if so.

I believe our existence in every layer is a reflection of the wider and greater cosmos in which we live. Every observable phenomenon in the cosmos is reflected in our existence. We are the microcosm of the macrocosm and our existence a repeating pattern of the same themes through every layer of social stratification and facet of existence. Just as there are extremes in the cosmos so we suffer from extremes here through nature and in our human existence. Just as there are dark places in the cosmos and some things we should stay away from as they will consume us to nothingness, equally so in our lives and human existence. Some become so powerful that they become a scourge on the rest. With the lesson that, when everything is just right, balanced, as our planet's distance from the sun, the so-called goldilocks zone, something beautiful can be created, our earth. Our challenge is simple in its basic premise, how to enjoy this place by creating balance in our cosmos.

Consequently,

PLEASE READ ON

5.1 "See past the facade.
Everything that is happening, from America to the UK, for
these are the protagonists, is designed to coerce us into a system.
A super system of surveillance, supreme power. They want
to be omniscient of your actions for who can subvert
the system if every individual is accounted for.
Then they have power, power to subvert and subjugate.
They can rule as they please.
They want power and nothing can be done to
stop them, for only a few see amongst many.
The "PROVERBIAL DICHOTOMY".
"THE PROVERBIAL DICHOTIC DILEMMA."

I still wonder how I came to the title of my book. However, reading over what I wrote at this point earlier on in my life, I realise that it was at this stage that I was starting to realise the function of the Dichotic Dilemma and how it permeated through all levels of existence. How it is, the fabric of life, an integral part of existence. It was at this stage that the principle was becoming realised in my mind and consciousness.

That principle is never more so vivid than as the piece above alludes to. Coming into the 21st century, Western dominance has been the defining factor, of at least and going beyond the last 100 years or so, as a phenomenon of recent global domination. The main protagonists, particularly in recent history, are America and England with America having the most determining influence. What happens in America is global news and at present, unsurprisingly so, they are the dominant economy on the world stock market. Consequently, it is to these places we look to as their dictates define, in many ways, the characteristics of the rest of the world.

This piece has distinct George Orwellian overtones as the Dichotic Dilemma is never more vivid than in the context of the capabilities of 21st century surveillance. To imagine these capabilities in the hands of undemocratic power institutions such as dictatorships and oligarchic power structures, it is a chilling thought to the possible state of human existence under such conditions. Although, it is not an impossible fate. Hence why our technological progression should be allied with a social progression in our politics, how we govern ourselves, distribute power and resources. If our technological progression outpaces our social and political progression, we might pay a penalty with our freedom and our lives. The basic instinct looms in our social and human existence and it manifests itself in ways that dominate us without us even realising it. The Dichotic Dilemma. Balance, we are doomed for the lack of it.

5.2 "Humanity today is the most selfish species.
We live on this earth as if we are its only inhabitants.
We have no respect for the other creatures, flora,
and fauna that co-habit this earth alongside us.
And the worst thing is such an idea in a public
forum would not be taken seriously by most but
would be ridiculed and laughed at and dismissed

on the premise that it is childish, naïve.
I would be seen as an idealistic hippie.
The Proverbial Dichotomy.
How sad.
However, this is only because the world is being dominated
by a society which thinks it knows all and thinks it has
increased the worth of a person but it has done no such thing.
People have been reduced to targets in the pursuit of
targets.
Expendable by products in the pursuit
of profits and self interests.
"COLLATERAL DAMAGE" in the pursuit of
valueless and hypocritical goals.
Our worth diminishes the more this system runs,
we think we are empowered but we are not.
Only a few have the real power.
Democracy is a sham and so is the notion
of justice, fairness and equality.
We unwittingly inflict misery upon each other through
the system as we try to survive and only a few enjoy
a "real" dividend from the suffering and pain.
However, these claims will still be dismissed as
pathetic, childish daydreams and a complete
naivety in acknowledging reality.
However that would only be a reflection of
the malignance of the cancer, the malice that
reigns over us with a bludgeoning mace.
Only a complete and utter overhaul will
do. A reboot of the system.
The earth to start afresh.
Rid itself of this pestilence that is the human race. Evil
took hold of the reins of power a time ago in history.

The Dichotic Dilemma

Took hold with a power so strong that
nothing has been able to offset it as it has spread
a malicious cancer all over the world.
Now the cancer is malignant and no effort
to try and restore what was, will do.
Nothing will be able to undo the damage that has
been done and restore truth and right knowledge as the
rightful leaders of the earth and all that inhabit it.
Only a complete overhaul will do as there is no way back.
Has humanity lost its way, or was this always the plan?
Where humanity would eventually find
itself? The system has corroded.
Nothing that is right stands in its glory.
Just ignorance and pestilence reign.
Only a complete overhaul."

Indeed a dramatic piece, a truly emotive reaction. We know cars pollute and yet we still drive. Success can even be measured by how many you can collect. Some of the extensively wealthy own collections of cars, material possessions just there to look at and soothe the ego, to boast of conquest. Depending on your perspective, some would look at this and see unbridled waste and immorality yet, should one not enjoy the fruits of their labour. New cell phones, iPads and televisions are out seemingly every day in our modern society. Yet if we do not buy, people lose their jobs and economies crumble. We seem doomed by our over reliance on oil yet oil is an integral part of almost every part of modern existence. We are now seemingly at the mercy of the system we have created. The money markets and the financial system, deterministic on the fate of whole nations. As the piece asks, has humanity lost its way or was this always the plan? Where technological and industrial discovery has led, we have followed. Subsequently, we have been trying to catch up with the consequences of the effects of that techno-industrial advance as we have learnt the consequences.

Deforestation, pollution and now we are in a fight to save the natural environment as we are so far gone down this route that it seems there is no way back. The natural world is integral to our existence on this planet as it contributes to the state of the biosphere yet it seems hopelessly at our mercy.

Some believe in doomsday prophecies and at present, there is some hysteria around the 2012 prophecies with regards to the belief in the Mayan calendar. Depending on your view on existence, where we are going and how we present as a race, with regards to our lesser attributes, sometimes one can feel that something has to give when observing emotionally. These doomsday predictions are reflective of a humanity in an emergency state of existence because in many ways our universal social existence is unbalanced and our nature is to seek balance. I do not fear death because it is an inevitable fate under any conditions. What I fear more is life, a whole existence under undesirable conditions. Hence, why people fear the apocalypse or apocalyptic scenarios, the fear of living under extremely undesirable conditions. However, we are fully capable of preventing this if we, as the piece suggests, overhaul our existential parameters and live as a race where we practise the positives of living as a family, as one race.

The human race. I believe that family means you are never alone. There are over 8 billion human beings on this planet, so why should we ever be alone!

We know volcanoes will erupt, there will be tornadoes, floods and other natural disasters depending on your proximity to such phenomena. It is not God's wrath. We live on an active planet. Our position and challenge is how to deal positively with these facts. It is so much harder to cope with the challenges of our planet when we expend more energy fighting ourselves. We are alienating ourselves from one another by valuing money over all else. Money over the human being, human life, and all life. If we continue to fight, be narrow- minded, individualistic in our groups, these apocalyptic worlds we fear will be our existence. As they are for the starving, the marginalised, and those living in war torn regions. Apocalypse happens every day whilst others, myself included, are fortunate enough at this time to drink fresh water and wait for the latest blockbuster film to come out and watch it in 3D whilst eating overpriced popcorn. There is no apocalypse coming except for the apocalypse we create for ourselves. Napalm, the hydrogen bomb, tomahawk missiles, the atomic bomb. That is the apocalypse of fear that we have created fighting ourselves.

Astronomers argue that our sun will not be extinguished for at least another few billion years. If our sun was ceasing to exist then yes, fear of the Armageddon and apocalypse would be fully justified. However, even just one billion years is long enough that such a fear should not even factor in our consciousness. What I see is human beings on this planet given full reign to live as they dictate in a bountiful and beautiful plane of existence. How and why, yes pertinent but inconsequential with regards to the fact that, WE ARE HERE. Yet we spend our time name calling and hating a sad indictment to our race. It all seems laughable in the context of everything else that abounds, the Universe at large in light of the existence we could have on this planet.

We are free to dictate our fate, only if we conquer what limits us, egotism, hate, corruption, selfishness, ignorance, lies, narrow-mindedness, our basic instincts. We have free will, absolute free will. Ours is just to understand its true meaning and its dictates. A balanced understanding that leads to its positive implementation.

5.3 *"It is amazing how words of kindness and words of affection to those dear and not so dear are difficult to say. Yet words of prejudice and malice flow easily like a stream flowing down a mountain slope."*

It is so much easier to hate and destroy than to be affectionate and understanding. Hate is a function of devolved thinking and love and understanding are functions of evolved thinking. Our failure to globally implement the positive aspects of the emotional spectrum is a function of our underdeveloped social existence. Openness and debate are the conduit towards better and higher thinking and realisations, the positive use of all our better evolved faculties including language, and cognitive capacity.

Destroying is so simple yet building asks of the best of ourselves with results truly breathtaking. What more a human society that is truly breathtaking.

5.4 *"Let your actions reflect what you say.*
For no man has the power to discern what
thoughts the other harbours.
We only have their actions as a guide. Therefore,
do not expect someone to know. Show, for we have
not the power to know, but the power to show.
It is in the actions, not the words."

Physical actions dictate outcomes. Our actions determine the world we live in. Positive thoughts, positive actions, positive outcomes.

5.5 *"You find "fulfilment" in shallow pursuits.*
You find "fulfilment" in the shallowest and most
meaningless activities. Mundane, your search.
You are so hollow, so vacuous.
I am not disparaging but I am truthful.
You know it's true because you know how you feel inside.
Open your eyes, wake up for you are just but a Zombie.
A zombie.

A zombie is an interesting concept. To be alive but brain dead or spiritually dead. We can and do go through life sometimes feeling void and empty. This is when spirituality becomes a very functional part of living a fulfilled existence. I believe emotions are a guide and how we feel informs us that something is missing. We find completeness and wholeness when we conquer negativity and partake in more fulfilling and wholesome activities. This is where moral teaching becomes a functional part of living as well. Standards, valuing yourself and your body and others as fulfilment can be found out of helping others. You can have all the money in the world but be alone and feel a void.

Showing that ultimately, it is other human beings that matter, not money and having a positive relationship with them. These values are the building blocks of a cohesive and positively functioning society.

Free Will means the human being is capable of any action and under poor guidance can do anything. Hence, that positive, wholesome, spiritual, and moral guidance is needed to inform the mind which induces and controls action of the important things in life which lead one not to feel vacuous but fulfilled. Breaking down the family and breaking down moral standards can lead to a broken down society and we can become like the zombies the piece denotes. Even so much as to prey on each other as we do chasing money and sustenance. Charity begins at home, as the adage and axiom declares. The nucleus, centre, and starting point where all aspects of life to be experienced outside of the family are inoculated into the developing mind. All that can be learnt in life can be learnt within the family unit so that when one goes out to see and meet the world, it is on a stable footing, mind, and emotional state. Humanity begins within the family unit and bond as are the human lessons and challenges, the nuclear reaction that goes out to affect the wider population either positively or negatively.

Morals dictate the highest standards so that deviation is not to an extreme. If the moral compass and footing is askew, then the degree of deviation is more so. Morality dictates that sex should be partaken in a bound commitment because it is the most functional method to cope with the consequences of sex; pregnancy and the resultant child welcomed into a stable and loving environment, sexually transmitted illnesses less a factor through the safety of monogamous sexual intercourse, wholesome pursuits, the more functional activities towards building a wholesome and positive humanity. That is the function of morality. Our basic urges and instincts mean we are capable of anything as we witness when morality and the rule of law are negated by the dictates of war and instability. The abhorrent atrocities chronicled as we pick up the pieces from strife.

We gain so much more by learning the value of others, applying positive morals and values as we pursue and perambulate the challenges of our existence.

5.7 *"Love is a fool's endeavour.*
Love is for anyone deluded enough to believe that
there is anything good, anything positive on this earth.
Loving is for those with a lot of time to waste.
A lot of energy to channel towards a
futile and fruitless endeavour.
Or is love for the wise, the strong, those not willing to give up?
Those willing to die with hope in the belief that
there is indeed something good, something positive,
something worth fighting and dying for.
Something worthwhile on this revolving sphere of uncertainty.
There is a truth to be found in these words but alas,
The "PROVERBIAL DICHOTOMY".
The everlasting "DICHOTIC DILEMMA".

Life's questions are myriad and complex, the presentation of the phenomenon a wondrous spectacle beguiling and bewildering. The sheer occurrence of the phenomenon is enough of a wonder to provide for a lifetime's contemplation. Extreme beauty and extreme tragedy are coexistent. The phenomenon of extremes. The Dichotic Dilemma. Yet here we are, plain as day. This being, this existence, intertwined.

To love, or to hate. Do we even have a choice? What is freedom, what is free will? Do they even exist? Yet I sit here tonight and write, a choice

I feel I have made, a choice I am making in spite of the deterministic forces that have led me here in this place and time.

Our challenge is great. Our challenges are great as individuals and as a human race. The forces that drive us are intrinsic and powerful. Yet at that point, that point of action, that point of utterance, the choic and the power to motion it is within the control of each and every single individual.

The Dichotic Dilemma

Chapter Six!!

The truth can seemingly be even more divisive than lies, so which would you rather have? The "DICHOTIC DILEMMA".

6.1 "Your humanity is judged on the basis of your skin tone......?????"

Ultimately, I argue, discuss, and debate as a member of the black race who are geographically centred as a stronghold in Africa. Our recent history coming into the 21st century is one that has left Africa, as an economic geographic location, lagging behind other parts of the world in terms of development, the prospects of future development and political stability enjoyed in the so-called first world. The continent of Asia is set to become potentially the dominant economic strong hold going into the 21st century. India is a rising economic and world power

whilst China, Japan, and Russia are established economic powers with China being the second largest economy in the world. At present, China's influence and economic activity is on the increase in Africa with little perceived return to the indigenous populations. It is discouraging to imagine another century of exploitation of the African continent with no significant return for the wider spread of its people and the resultant future for the normal man, woman, and child in Africa.

The Dichotic Dilemma

The issues are still the same as they have always been. The imbalance of trade, the need to rebalance a recent history of exploitation and the need for stable political governance that represents the interests of the people. Less dictatorships and more democratic governance.

Democracy as a political concept and ideal does more to abate the corruptible nature of human beings once ascended to power and allows for plurality of opinions and fairer appointments into positions of influence. Africa and Africans do not need charity, they are human beings, able, and capable to master their own destinies. It is again discouraging to imagine another century of Oxfam and Red Cross advertising campaigns depicting the suffering and destitution of, in most cases, black Africans.

The continent and a large number of its peoples are paying the price for the natural abundance of their geographical location's resources. Whilst to some degree, it is fair to say that the former colonial masters through the legacy of colonisation enjoy and benefit from the imbalance of trade. It is sobering to hypothesise that perchance, by the virtue of a miraculous fluke, if all the black Africans in Africa woke up white in complexion, this imbalance could be redressed. Could things be different? A thought.

Simple skin tone.

Colonisation brought westernisation and a western infrastructural framework of existence. As the indigenous peoples naturally fought for their worth as human beings to be recognised, the colonial masters withdrew and in some cases along with the infrastructural struts that hold together western civilisation. Hence, a lot of African countries and peoples are caught between worlds, one old and one new and are languishing as other parts of the world progress.

Indeed, human beings have always fought over resources. Chance, coincidence, and natural selection mean some people find themselves in locations of abundant natural reserve and opportunity whilst some do not. Consequently, the other always has what the other wants and our devolved social capacity means we fight to protect our own interests. Why not prosper together?

The world is ours, us all. Not some more than others. Us all

6.2 *"What is it that creates anarchy and lets it reign?*
Lets anarchy reign over the innocent?
Allows another man to spit in another's face?
Urinate and defecate all over another's pride and honour
and allow the other to have no power to overturn?
Except the power to capitulate, to bow down and beg for mercy.
Then find peace and solitude in being an eternal object of pity
and disdain whilst the perpetrator has no honour at all?
Who is he that justifies such a situation?
What is it that thinks it has power to allow such a state?
Who or what is it that entitles itself the
power to justify such a state of affairs?
No explanation will do for me, for I see no reason.
But, who am I to ask such a question?
For in this world I am just a black man after all.
But I say, I entitle myself the power to say, "YE WITH POWER, YE WITH POWER ABOVE ALL, YE WITH POWER I BESEECH YOU AND SAY, YE WITH POWER, QUESTION YOURSELVES."

This poem takes me back to a time of great anger, angst, pain and disillusionment. My natural urge was to find answers to questions and presentations of existence that were greatly representative of the strife of human existence. This particular poem was in response to my perceptions of the AIDS epidemic and my perceived origins of the disease. An epidemic which in many ways, is evidently crippling the populations where it is concentrated which lack adequate medical intervention. It creates orphans and depletes a potential workforce and inhibits the development of strong and stable societies in those regions particularly in some parts of Africa. As a black Zimbabwean and Southern African by birth where there is a high incidence of the illness, this fact is and was particularly poignant to me as displayed in the piece.

In a time of distinct racial separation in my mind, it caused me great anger at the notion, as suggested in some communities, of the thought that AIDS was an imported iatrogenic virus by western dictates. The exact origins of the illness is a disputed subject with many schools of thought however, at this stage in my life I was more akin to the iatrogenic argument as the source origin of the illness through a supposed polio vaccination campaign. I remember folk music which seemed to suggest that this great agent of death did not exist before the white man came to our lands. Reflective of humanity and its torturous history and destructive potential. One shudders at the thought of the likes of Josef Mengele, Auschwitz concentration camp doctor who experimented savagely on human beings. Our deepest and darkest depths.

The greatest threat and danger of humanity from itself is our intelligence under ignorant, misguided and erroneous ideals. Highlighting the necessity of Eclecticism in our approach to existence. Our ability to have erroneous intentions and ideals and being able to fulfil and follow them through by virtue of intelligence and free will. We are coming from a period of great overt racial prejudice in some cases very extreme as in Apartheid South Africa. I remember as a child through my curiosities reading through literature that testified to the hate of some of the South African white human beings for black human beings. Some so much so that they were bent on the annihilation of the black race. Allied with the human capacity for intelligence, one shudders at the possibilities.

In my earlier years in England during my psychology lessons at high school, I was the only black person in my class, and remember learning that some experiments and clinical trials in the past into the effects of drugs and illnesses were conducted on black people. There are some places as human beings where we just must not go, no matter the pretext or context.

"YE WITH POWER, YE WITH POWER ABOVE ALL, YE WITH POWER I BESEECH YOU AND SAY, YE WITH POWER, QUESTION YOURSELVES."

When a human being starts to operate under a perspective in which the value of others is diminished, the value of things outside their objectives is diminished, that and those human beings are capable of anything.

As we move towards the future in light of the savagery of history, it pains to even suggest the pain of progress. It pains to even propose, the Dichotic Dilemma.

6.3 "It is foolishness to believe what you cannot validate for yourself.
Especially when the message is coming from a
non-accountable source, an untrustworthy
source, a malevolent source.
It is utter foolishness."

An ignorant mind is a dangerous mind.

6.4 "Knowledge is power.
Knowledge is the key.
The key to unlock the gate into a parallel Universe.
A different dimension, an alternate existence.
A different paradigm of existence.
It is the key to understanding the façade.
The prevailing dynamic that is life as we see it today.
For this life is the paragon of confusion, an
endless riddle of unanswered questions.
Things always seem to be upside down.

*The wrong way around, inverted and positioned
in the way they should not be.
An ETERNAL knowledge, a RIGHT
knowledge, a UNIVERSAL knowledge.
A knowledge to lift the heavy iron blanket of
confusion that presides over a people.
A knowledge.
A key to consciousness. A key to unlock the truth.
The key to unlocking, unlocking THE PURPOSE
OF LIFE."*

The purpose of life. Maybe too far a question, but one can only suggest. All feels well and right when everything is balanced. We have to find that balance. Understand it and exist by it.

*6.5 "Do others just accept the reality that is in front of
them?
You have to "step" over others to get ahead.
A real man is one who can "provide" for his "family".
A rich man who gives them "everything" they want
even though he steps over everyone else to get there?
Little wonder the world is the way it is because every
"real man" is stepping over the other to get ahead.
Everyone is looking after their own interests.
Or, is a "real man" someone who is going to strive to
always do the right thing.
Love with all his heart and be trodden on by all, even
by those he loves the most and have his heart broken,
but still stand?
Then get no recognition and have "nothing", be
"no one" amongst other men because he is not a rich
man.*

Then be deemed incapable and get no adulation.
Whilst the other man gets all the praise and glory which
he has achieved through his malicious actions. The
weight of being a good man in a world full of evil men
is almost unbearable, if not impossible to carry.
Yet again, THE PROVERBIAL DICHOTIC DILEMMA
The battle between good and evil.
The seemingly impossible task of being a good
person in this very cruel and cold world.

6.8 "It is so simple, knowledge is understanding.
For how can you understand if you do not know? How
can you be quick to shun what you do not Understand?
There could be good in it.
You are the proponent of ignorance. Seek knowledge first.
For knowledge leads to understanding.
But the right knowledge can yet lead to an even better
understanding and hence a better outcome.
Knowing yes, knowledge yes.
They knew how to make an atom bomb
and look at the outcome.
Knowledge yes, but right knowledge better yet and
ever more, the knowledge to be humble."

Ability gives rise to the ego and the human ego is that thing we always have to battle against. The desire to be dominant and self preserve.

Being humble means always understanding, in a balanced way, your ability to achieve what you can and equally so, others inability to do so. When you are at the top, it is your greatness that leads the way for those below you so they can follow.

The human being can, but at times, that does not mean "do." Humbleness is a function of understanding. Humbleness means, when you are strong, respect the weak and when you are weak, respect the strong. Therein, the necessity and importance of both is understood.

6.10 *"Know your adversary my black sister, know your*
adversary.
Your primary adversary is the white woman
for she is confusing your men.
Her very nature is making your men lose interest in
you.
He has no time for you anymore because you
value yourself and he is choosing to drink the cheap
wine that has caused him to be drunk and poisoned
till he does not even know who or what he is.
Your secondary adversary is the white man.
For he is subjugating and taking away the pride of your men.
He is making them weak and have no confidence in themselves.
They cannot support their homes anymore and have
no direction leaving your children destitute.
The white man is also surreptitiously injecting
your men and yourself with an even more sinister
poison that is rendering us all as a people mentally
and physically destitute, beaten and broken.
All this is leaving you to fend for yourself as your men
are incapacitated right now.
For they are being attacked on two fronts
rendering them both weak and confused.
If one does not get them, the other will and you just bear the
brunt of the confusion and at times you get confused as well.
But you are strong, you have always been.
We are still here because of you.

You are still producing soldiers and raising them by yourself.
Against all the odds and the most ardent of
adversity you still persevere and prevail.
For you are strong, you are our survival.
Yet for what, I do not know.
However, for your effort you deserve a
prize at the end of the road.
For such a struggle has to be worth a prize.
This message is for the real "black women" still
standing out there.
Your struggle is being noticed.
It has to be, somewhere, our struggle as a forsaken people.
For if not, then the very effort is the height of
purposeless and senseless futility."

A poem that speaks of a time of subjugation. Hate creates hate. I do not want to live in a world that causes people to see these visions and have such opinions of each other. I fear my own thoughts as I read this and wonder where my consciousness was that I could view the world in such a manner. Such vicious perceptions of one another do not bode well for humankind. These are the perceptions of a mind at war, a man at war and in war, no one wins.

When the mind is under the right influence, it sees a better world and can consequently, conceive a better world. If the mind sees enemies, there will be war. When the mind sees a common thread, there will be understanding.

6.11 "All you do is politick, I just want to live.
Yet, all you do is politick.
I was born into this world, I still do not know why. I
was born a black man, I still do not know why.
But all you do is politick. That is all you ever do.

Promise! Promise! Promise!
Delivering an attribute to you is ever so
foreign. Who gave you that right?
Who gave you that right over me?
You do not have my interests at heart.
Being black, you definitely do not have my interests at heart.
Why do I not have power over myself?
Why should I be a subject?
It remains to be seen.

Many themes are discussed in this piece. However, most of all in this piece is the idea of politics. Politics, our systems of human governance. There are many schools of thought as to what is the best set of political ideals to allow for optimal human political satisfaction with the power structure. This piece just reflects frustration with politics and politicians as we all are at some point in our lives.

However, it is clear to note that the overriding political position of the land affects how people experience their existence. Most importantly, what the overriding dictates of the political system are will reflect the general behaviour of the population. It amazes me when looking at power structures of governance how the ideas of a few can have such a determinant effect on human life. Power truly is that thing to be most cautious of and managed by our highest ideals by the virtue of its overbearing effect on life and the life experience on this planet, biosphere, earth.

Case and point, when racism was permissible by law and supported by the political structure, it was practised on the streets, equally so, when it was abolished, its influence naturally receded. On the same basis, global politics is about each country looking after its own interests by and large. Under that paradigm and political perspective, real cohesive global human existence is difficult to achieve. Each country fends for itself as humanity is divided by arbitrary lines.

The necessity for different countries can be argued for on the basis that

it creates order, as a way of effectively managing human movement, life, resources, and protecting territories. However, ultimately, a country is a body of self-interest when, in the grandest observation, the human race is one. Borders, zones, and demarcations mean the suffering of the other, or your neighbour, is their own suffering. It is curious how, as human beings, we only discover our humanity through times of crisis and disaster. When an earthquake or floods occur for example, that is when we all become human beings and see the need for helping others and living cohesively. When there is a car accident or a fire, that is when we discover our humanity. The rest of the time, we seem at odds through perceived demarcations which clearly become less distinct in times of crisis. They should not exist.

It is not impossible to functionalise a global human existence. With centralised food stores for the community, education centres so every mind is full of knowledge, industrial zones for building projects and housing maintenance, technological and health centres all over the globe with no territorial lines, Pangea is a global human coexistive alliance. Yet, our political rhetoric and outlook is about fending for our

own countries and amassing wealth for our own people, ourselves, when we are all the same. A lot of time, energy, and valuable resources are used creating weapons and security systems to protect and keep those who create them safe from their "enemies". I recently saw a newspaper magazine cover titled, *The Future of War.* A future of war? Who are we fighting against? There are only human beings, animals, plants, microbes and inanimate objects on this planet. So who are we fighting against apart from ourselves because we live divided?

Who will we be fighting in this future of war? The African continent has human beings on it. The Eurasian continent has human beings on it.

North and South American continents have human beings on them. Oceania and Antarctica have human beings on them. Who are we fighting against?

We need to advance ou ics as we our technology. Else, the children in the e oo wr *was born into this world, I still do not*

know why.

I was born a black man, I still do not know why.

But all you do is politick.

If the stomach is sated, there is no need to steal, beyond that, it is greed and foolishness. Morality teaches against that. However, when the stomach is empty, all the rules cease to exist.

We can feed every mouth on this planet, yet all the lines that divide us as nations and as people mean we only want to feed ourselves. Hence, we fight.

At one point, globalisation seemed a curse and a scourge, yet, a singular vision of human coexistence and interconnectedness erodes the demarcation lines which means a foe becomes a friend. If we are reliant on and supportive of each other for our survival, we cease to shoot, kill, and steal. A world, not of excess for some and inadequacy for others, but a balanced world. Where a human being can contribute then be able to enjoy this beautiful foliage, family, and friends.

A new politics for a new world. A 21st-century world of technological and human social advance born from and balanced against a savage history. A developed and democratic human planet, not in competition but co existence.

21st-century politics.

6.12 *"Society functions on consensus.*
But the truth is the truth and consensus is consensus.

*They are not one, they are not the same,
they are two separate entities.
Consensus is functional, but the truth is the truth."*

What I glean from this piece echoes the preceding theme from the piece above. We have so many different societies around the world, hence very different points of view. This is where the inability to coexist globally comes from. Going to these different societies is like going to another world completely by virtue of the difference in the phenomenon of human existence there. These societies will have their own consensus and rules by which they pursue their existence. The same applies in the grander scheme of observation and in the individual experiences of life we have. Different families and different people within those families will have different views.

Hence, ultimately, different societies consequently have different consensus and this is where global misunderstanding occurs. I write in the piece that consensus is consensus but the truth is the truth.

Consensus is the agreement that works and is beneficial to the people involved in that agreement.

Hence, Consensus could be racial hatred, but the truth is always the value of each human being. Consensus could be the raping of women, but the truth is always the value of each human being. Consensus could be an imbalance in trade laws favouring conquering nations over the conquered but the truth is always the value of each human being.

Consensus could be the conscription of child soldiers but the truth is always the value of each human being. Consensus could be tribalism but the truth is always the value of each human being. Consensus could be a system which allows some to be billionaires and be profligate with that return whilst others starve but the truth is always the value of each human being. Consensus could be the importance of just profit but the truth is always the value of each human being. Consensus could be exploitation but the truth is always the value of each human being.

Consensus could be practicality but the truth is always the value of each human being. Consensus could be the importance of the financial cost over the human and social cost but the truth is always the value of each human being. Consensus could be atheism or theism or polytheism but the truth is always the value of each human being. Consensus could be Orthodox or Protestant but the truth is always the value of each human being. Consensus could be Christianity or Islam but the truth is always the value of each human being. Consensus could be war, but the truth is always the value of each human being. Consensus could be individualism but the truth is always the value of each human being.

Right wing or left wing views, but the truth is always the value of each human being.

Our consensus should always be the value of each human being at all times, at all places, in all ways. Serve yourself or humanity. Indeed, The Dichotic Dilemma.

6.14 "Rationality is a function of consensus"

Hence, our rationality should always be the value of each human being at all times, at all places in all ways.

6.15 "No one loves war like they do.
No one loves anarchy like they do.
No one profits and has profited from pain
and bloodshed like they do and have.
All they do is exhaust their energy on things
that bring pain, misery, and death.
Their advancement is analogous with destruction,
for the more they advance, the more destruction
looms and suffering for others intensifies.
They celebrate and make merry as others weep. We

cannot be the same, we cannot be brothers.
Because brothers are family and family shares in each
other's suffering.
A brother suffers when his brother suffers.
They are the architects of death and destruction
and they marvel at their ability to destroy.
And as they build for themselves, they destroy for others.
Their selfishness and greed knows no bounds.
What they deem to be clever is foolishness.
For it bears no principle, logic or "TRUTH" in it.
Only a truth and a principle that can only ultimately destroy.
It is not wisdom to build something that can destroy
everything before us, the atomic bomb.
You have dabbled in the forbidden arts
and now we shall all pay the price.
You have opened Pandora's box when you know you
should not and an ugly serpent has come out. A villainous
and poisonous serpent that shall strike with no mercy.
Napalm, ballistic missiles, the hydrogen bomb,
tanks, guns, bullets, arms.
No one loves war like they do and it pays them richly.
However, the innocent pay an even dearer price.
It is not wisdom to only think of today.
To loot and plunder and exploit the earth and others
in the hope of profiting from immediate gains.
Forgetting that there is a tomorrow that spans over a million
years to come and the future of those generations to consider.
It is not wise to live without "PRINCIPLES"
because principles preserve.
They teach of limits and boundaries.
This is a knowledge the unprincipled lack.
They find chivalry in fighting, but what

The Dichotic Dilemma

they fight for is selfish and conceited.
Their progress is like a vile and cancerous tissue,
progressing towards malignance and the
eventual destruction of everything.
Their knowledge is a knowledge of destruction
and they are our teachers for we read from their
books and attend their institutes of learning.
So what are we learning?
They have taken us away from our ways and told us they
are stupid and "primitive" and taught us their own.
Now we are confused and trapped in their vice-like grip.
Theirs is a knowledge of subjugation, greed, power and for
some unforeseeable reason, no one has power to stop them.
Only the power to join them if not perish.
There must have been a way, a better
way. A time, a better time.
There must have been understanding or there shall be,
for it is the way of the Universe to attain a balance.
Positive and negative, right and wrong, up and down, left
and right, black and white, one has to have the other.
Therefore, before confusion, suffering and pain
must have been the invariable alternate.
Where there are lies, elsewhere must be truth.
I fail, I fail, please truth show yourself.
This confusion pains me, this life tortures me, their
anarchy, their anarchy rattles my very soul.
Answers, come forth.
Knowledge, open my eyes so I can see, so I can
see for myself the reason for such a state.
Their idea of power, white power is founded on the
principles of hate, subjugation, and superiority.
Our idea of power, black power is founded on the

principles of freedom and belief in ourselves.
Theirs is to hate, that is their knowledge.
It is so deep-seated that they do not even see it. They
think it is their right, and they are justified to look
down upon others because they are lesser beings.
They are selfish and dream of utopias where
they eliminate everyone but themselves.
Their selfishness knows no bounds for they also dream
of eliminating their own weak, in this utopia.
All in the bid to make the "perfect" race with "perfect" people.
They call this selfish act, eugenics.
To eliminate so-called faulty genes so everyone is to
required specifications, designer babies and the like,
so everyone is "perfect".
Who made you God?
Why can you not see the beauty in incongruity? Your
plans lack principles and they are bound to backfire.
They know not that love, kindness, and
compassion can be found in weakness.
This is not their knowledge, for their knowledge
is spawned from selfishness and hate.
What reason do the fair have for hating the darker ones?
Since our paths crossed through history, theirs has been
to desecrate, demolish, demoralise, dominate, and
devastate everything they touched, including people.
If you do not believe me, ask the countless dead
slaves, red Indians, Eskimos or Inuits, if you wish, the
Inca, the Maya, the Maori, and the Aborigines
in Australia.
The victims of apartheid and colonialism.
The victims of racial segregation.
However, above all, ask the earth.

*See what it thinks of this new system they introduced to the world, the Capitalist system. For they saw gold and saw how it can make them rich so they turned it into money.
They have been robbing the earth of all its minerals and digging, excavating and deforestation, all in the name of "progress" and "civilisation".
Now look at the earth and humanity today and see if we really have been civilised.
Or were it the ancient civilisations who lived within their means and worshipped the land and animals for they respected them?
Look and assess for yourself who is more civilised.
For it is not because they were not intelligent. Look at the structures they built, we still do not know and understand how they did it till this day even with all this "technology".
The pyramids in Egypt and South America.
The Hieroglyphics, the gold which can be found in the tombs.
The Great Zimbabwe monuments which are built of stone with no mortar or cement but have conquered the test of time.
They knew how to make all these things, but they perceived life from a different knowledge base.
The white man saw this gold and has taken it from these places, from Africa like it was his birthright. A wealth of knowledge has been lost in the transition of time.
For as I write this, I long to know what my ancients knew.
To see what they saw with their eyes, for I am blind to this as our lineage has been broken.
Now today we live in a world of debt for that is what seems to be the purpose of life now.
To work and pay off debts.
All to appease the system and its protagonists.*

We are threatened by what they have
created. The world knows no peace.
Ask the depleted Amazon rainforest.
The natives to it have lived with it for a very long time and
they respected the balance and lived life in a way to sustain it.
However, in just over a century, it has been depleted
in order to sustain the industrial world.
The white man's world, the Capitalist world.
The result of which is that our actions today are
going to have direct and consequential
effects on the future generations.
For it will be because of how we live life today that
they inherit an earth which cannot sustain them.
All because we have lived and worshipped a system which does
not respect the earth because it is selfish and without principles.
However, for most of us, we have just found ourselves in
a situation the rest is up to powers beyond ourselves.
However, we still need to ask ourselves the question,
"What am I going to do to make a difference?"
If you stand alone, the world can seem unconquerable.
But standing together in unison, no task is too great.
An individual contribution from everyone
makes for a monumental achievement.
Yet you still hear that America will not sign
agreements to cut down on their greenhouse
emissions yet they are the highest contributor
of greenhouse gases into the atmosphere.
Everywhere they have gone, they have taken the aborigines
out of their ancient existence, subjugated them, miseducated
them using their own brand of "Christianity".
Yet they claim to have civilised us and we
owe them for teaching us to "read" and speak

English for that has made us civilised?
Everywhere they have gone, they have left a
catastrophic trail of destruction and suffering.
They put a lot of things out of balance for
they have no respect for nature.
In their eyes, they were building an empire and exploring.
You have built your empire but at what price?
Of course, you do not know because you enjoy off
the opulence you have pillaged, whilst we, the
unfortunate, suffer, so "WE" know the price.
You have blood on your hands and a debt to pay. Oh, the
pain of mis-education, it stings with a relentless sting.
Their education is capitalism.
They hate communism and the world is at war
because of their so-called civilisation.
This unforgiving capitalist system.
They made us bare and everything that
prevails today is because of them.
They lie so much they believe their own lies. Nothing you read
in the papers or see in the news is the real truth of events.
We live under a heavy blanket of lies and
mis-education so that those in power can maintain
their place.
To what end?, I say.
A person depending on your skin colour, geographical
situation, and fortune or misfortune is only alive
on this earth for a finite period of time.
So what is the point of all this we go
through when we are on this earth?
There has to be a significant purpose. How
can another person be a monkey?
We all communicate so those who call others monkeys

*and apes have to be monkeys and apes as well.
Else, how do we communicate in the same exact way?
Their ignorance is staggering and ignorance
is the mother of destruction.
So they destroy.
They destroy everything and all that is left is for them to destroy
themselves and in doing so they will take us with them.
Why are we so weak? Why are we so weak?
Why have we no power, no power at all?
Why have I no power at all to make a difference
except the power to write on a paper?
A fragile piece of paper that can ignite and combust
and take my soul and everything I hold dear with
it in a dark and sorrowful cloud of smoke.
Who are you, who are you, ye who torments those
who do not know why they are tormented?
They have destroyed many a people
chasing their selfish ambitions.
A genocide history is left behind like they were
worthless.
The red Indians for example. How cruel are you, sun?
How cruel are you to rise and continue to do so? Continue
to do so and kiss the earth with the warm beautiful
smile of your never-ending rays from an unknown
place and act as if there is no suffering that happens,
has happened and will happen here on this earth?
For everyday to come and go like there is peace on earth.
How cruel are you?
Now, either my black brother is locked up,
African, infected with AIDS, infected with mental
poison, it is a wonder we are still here.
To what end, I say, to what end?*

To what end when just beyond the sky is a whole
different dimension that we do not know about?
Why are we so bound to this earth's surface?
Why have we not the power to just lift off and
fly into the clouds and beyond the sky?
Leaving all the suffering and killing and malice that goes on.
Why have we got to be bound to this earth surface
when there is a whole other Universe beyond
our sky that we do not know about?
Why are we so bound when we could just
fly away and leave the suffering?
To what end?, I say.
Our suffering and toil on this earth seems so
isolated and insignificant in relation to the
Universe out there whilst we are stuck here.
To what end?, I say.
There is a whole galaxy out there.
Yet here we are subject to the foolish, the
inconsiderate and the malicious.
Yet there is a whole galaxy out there. To what end?, I say.

This piece is the culmination and summation of all that frustrated me, all that I saw and all that I felt. It tells a tale of pain, confusion, and bewilderment. The anguish of the struck. A young man's view of the world at a time when he still had a lot to learn and a lot to see but burned with seemingly unanswerable questions. To what end?, I say.

The truth can be a bitter pill to swallow and life can seem a never-ending tragedy and trial. I swallowed the pill and asked the questions and today I see a better vision of the world than what I saw at that time when my consciousness was ravaged with emotional pain. Where I once saw only race and believed them separate, now I see the human being.

I see the human being and its very long history from origins still inconclusively substantiated but present nonetheless. I see the human being in a universal space, a Universe whose origins are still inconclusively substantiated but present nonetheless. I see similarity in the grandeur and apparent void of this universal space with the grandeur and apparent void of this human being and existence. I see the extremes of the human being and the extremes of the universal space. I see now the potential for a bright future and the potential for a dark future and the human being the singular conduit to determine which, individually and as a collective. I see now the danger and the unbelievable opportunity of free will. I see the challenge of survival. I see the Dichotic Dilemma and ultimately I see balance, its necessity and function.

What I cannot see is the world beyond, naturally so. The conclusion then being, what matters is the world here and now, today and tomorrow with the past a permanent spectre forever dwindling into antiquity, a teacher and a guide, always whispering the lessons that should be taken forward and the tragedies that should be left behind.

The truth is a tter pill to swal w but some say the truth will set y free. Freedom is an opportunity d a challenge to bring out and make the best of ourselves against all that could make us monsters. The Dichotic Dilemma.

Chapter Seven!!

The Conundrum Of Human Existence.
A Phenomenon Most Fascinating.
A Phenomenon Most Intriguing.

I am twenty-six years old now, turning twenty-seven in a few months time. It seems like only a few years ago I was in Zimbabwe starting high school thinking, wow, four years from now, I will be in form four as we called it, 16 years of age generally. I remember relaxing and thinking, wow, I have all the time in the world till then, that is ages away. Yet here I am, twenty-six years of age now, in Reading, England, sitting in front of a laptop, looking through my window and seeing a virgin hot air balloon floating away.

I have had a very average and mundane day and I think I am having a bit of a midlife crisis. I am not yet married, and I am looking for love again. I am pondering on my career prospects and have desires of furthering my current station but am not really sure how I am going to do so and get there. I have written this book and am not really sure what to make of it, its relevance, notability or whether it is going to remain what it has always initially been, a personal expression to understand my life. At this stage, I have an overwhelming feeling of everything just is and that is all there is to it. I am just acutely aware that I am a human being.

Yet, without a shadow of a doubt, right now, as I write, galaxies exist in places we might never see. The sun is out there somewhere, a million light years away burning ferociously in a magnificent fireball that gives us here warm sunny days to enjoy a barbecue. Kate Middleton is out there somewhere maybe waving at someone. Barack Obama is maybe thinking about a speech. Someone is getting robbed. Someone is planning a holiday.

There are starving people in some neglected part of the world. Someone has just made a million dollars and the meaning of existence for them has instantaneously transformed. Someone has lost their baby in childbirth. The moon is there, where it always is. In Syria, there is civil unrest as the balance of power, fate, and destiny is favouring some and not others. A lion is on the hunt. My blood is coursing through my body and unbelievable chemical processes are happening to make me be what I am right here and now.

The conundrum of human existence,
a phenomenon most fascinating,
a phenomenon most intriguing.

I like to think I am a philosopher maybe. Self proclaimed, maybe so. I also like to believe that I have a mainly politico-socio mind and it is on this basis that I will drive home my final summations.

I have discussed a lot of subjects in this book, cohesively, I hope. Information and knowledge gained through observation and information-gathering from many sources. I believe it is possible that there is something to be learnt and observed from every single phenomenon of existence. Ultimately, that is my source, and my initial point of learning was my pain. Emotional pain and confusion that characterised greatly, the earlier years of my existence. Hence, the need to attempt to understand the necessity of human suffering.

The building blocks of life are invisible to the human eye yet they are the basis on which all physical life matter and phenomena exist. The presence of animate creatures starts from the microscopic and from this most basic form of existence we originate. Simple cellular structures bonding, differentiating, and slowly developing into our more identifiable physical form. From within the body of another human being we grow and develop, the complications of life and survival already taking their full course until we are fully delivered into this plane of physical human existence. Some prematurely so, and the rest, in differing ways unleashed to the full gamut of the challenge of human social existence in a biosphere full of other non-human creatures.

The conundrum of human existence,
a phenomenon most fascinating,
a phenomenon most intriguing.

To argue against intelligent design seems naive and narrow minded. Yet, as human beings, we become the whole full range to live any form of life in a world as complex as the Universe beyond. Some truly positive lives where the full abundance of human existence can be enjoyed and some truly negative a story of trial and pain. How this can occur, we are fully aware.

That said, what is without doubt or question is that through our lives, we have an impact on the lives of others. Once here, we have the ability to shape the structure of our existence. Human suffering is real, and it is a direct consequence of how we impact others along with the challenges of survival.

Then the call becomes as ever, good governance, good principles, and balance in the way we implement our ideals. Always being aware that the things that make us the strongest, are also the things that we are most threatened by. Hierarchical structures and conformity give order so things can run smoothly, yet they are also the means by which great tragedies occur as poor ideals are transferred through the hierarchy enforcing negative actions. The Dichotic Dilemma.

All the knowledge and ability we need to facilitate a positive existence is available to us now through history and time. We have enough insight now into the nature of our lesser characteristics and their source.

Building a positive environment for human existence will produce a positive humanity. Can we answer this call?

It wasn't enough in my mind to conclude that the world was bad because there were a lot of evil people and the devil was the cause of evil. That would be then concluding that equally, there are a lot of good people. However, I realised that it is not that simple. Consequently, I concluded that there are human beings and that it is exactly when others think they are better and their worth overrides that of others where the imbalance and trouble starts. Instead of trying to understand and appreciate, the function becomes dominating and shunning.

Furthermore, it was to realise that the contributing factors to our existence and behaviours went much deeper than the simpler idea of good and evil. There were intrinsic contributory factors. An observation from the inside out. From the minute to the above and beyond. Intrinsic and extrinsic.

Through a naturally questioning mind, I had to develop a new perspective and format of looking at the world and existence. My conclusion has been this, The Dichotic Dilemma. An intrinsic idea to understand human beings and human existence through the function of my own personal emotional turmoil. Who are we, what are we, what is evil, what is good, how can they be quantified in the context of the complexity of the human being and existence? Who is evil, who is good, yet we seemingly are, some more than others. I believe evil is an extreme level of functional or pragmatic thinking where empathy is devolved and other animate creatures are reduced to objects and obstacles and their spiritual value is nullified. Therein as ever is the crux of the issue, functionality to sustain our existence, individually and as a collective against the need to maintain a spiritual perspective of the world around us. Spirituality means we create a value to all that is around us where the body is not just a body but an entity. The earth, flora, and fauna are here with us and necessary for our existence. Are we just flesh or spirit?, the truth is certainly somewhere in between. It is when we reduce that emotive value of those around us that we begin to create a world of conflict as opposed to otherwise a world and existence that could be better.

What is clear is that, for every phenomenon of existence, there will always be at least two alternative views to it. That is our point of conflict but should be our point of understanding. It is amazing to think of the many people who spend a lifetime in oppression by the virtue of having an alternate view point on the micro to macro societal scale.

We have enough of a challenge contending with the nature of ourselves and the constraints of survival. Yet when we improve our living conditions, we are better placed to deal with these challenges and realise the better aspects of existence. We need a system of redistribution and money seems to be the most effective and functional system. However, it is fair to say, as soon as a monetary value is attached to something, the context and meaning of that thing changes. How much is food worth, how much is family worth, how much is love worth, how much is life worth? As ever, the Dichotic Dilemma. What makes us strong can also cripple us. Practicality and pragmatism against the higher principles, and therein lies the challenge. When we run away from our challenges and choose the less-principled route, we miss a moment of raised understanding. Balance. Coexistence between positive and negative, two sides of the spectrum.

As money seemingly is the most effective form of resource redistribution, I believe that no one person on this planet should be paid more than a threshold amount. Equally so, no one should be paid below a threshold amount. It is clear to see that vast disparities in opulence are what create and contribute greatly to human strife. If all a human being needs to survive is food, shelter, and water, the rest is in addition, and beyond that is excess. I believe people who make greater contributions should indeed be rewarded, that is fairness and positively encourages competition. However, it should not be to the detriment of others. A monetary cap on levels of remuneration means the rest of the money can be redistributed to society, schools, and hospitals, for example. The result being that every school and hospital and other human amenities are of world standard. We need to eliminate elitism and social class but naturally be aware and respectful that the depth of others' contributions can seemingly outstrip those of others, yet everyone's contribution is important. Is an architect more important than a waste collector? We need a humanity where each individual has an equal chance and does not belong to a class but makes a contribution to society. In return, society looks after everyone and we can enjoy our planet.

It is obscene and a sad indictment of our species that unimaginable levels of wealth belong to some and when abject poverty befalls others. Are we, as proposed by others, the most evolved beings or, as by others, the children of God when we facilitate such an existence? A balanced world is achievable with a philosophical and political change in our ideologies. Failing that, the question then is, what are we and what does it mean to be a human being and human beings?

If everyone enjoys a fair standard of living and is included into society on the basis of equal human respect globally, all the things we fear will at least abate. Destitution, war, immigration, all products of global social imbalance. A mundane point would be to say, no one needs more than a million pounds or dollars a year to survive. In essence, one individual only needs a certain amount of resources to consume individually to sustain themselves or live comfortably. The rest should be used to fix a broken planet and a broken humanity to serve only yourself or to serve others, better yet, to serve yourself and others, positive application of our power, understanding, and abilities, conquering our lesser selves. Balance. My personal belief is of a world without money and everyone just contributes however their talent presents to a universal human existence. Again, all one truly needs is food, water, shelter, and the presence of others.

It is good to dream. Indeed it is. You need the dream first. There are those who distinctly believe in an afterlife. Personally, I find it difficult to believe in things that cannot be proven, or seen.

Consequently, what I find most pertinent is improving and valuing more the life here for this is what we can prove and see, in its splendour and brutality at times. Misguided ideals and principles are a fundamental contributor to the brutality. Yet out of great strife can come great triumph. That is certainly the hope for our species and at times, the individual story of life.

For whatever reason, whatever causal and confluential factors, we have a space within which to lucidly and independently exist. We are at a time of great understanding and great power in terms of our ability to manipulate the elements. Yet we seem to be more oriented towards the financial cost and gain as opposed to the human and planetary cost and gain. You are governed by your fundamental principles and you will reap the results of your beliefs.

I believe in the human being but we are subject to laws just like everything else. In extreme circumstances, we react and behave extremely and become all the things we fear. In balanced circumstances, we have more balanced lives. Balanced morals, politics, laws, systems of governance, systems of redistribution. A balanced world will lead to a balanced human existence. What is clear is that we live and we die. Life has a different meaning for all of us, yet the fundamental attributes and principles of existence are the same.

However, ultimately, we have one planet and one race. If we live as one, we definitely will see a better day so we do not have to wait for the afterlife which may or may not exist. The Dichotic Dilemma.

In light of the functional and practical challenges of being human beings, when discussing humanity and existence, I believe it is always right to espouse the highest ideals. This has been my attempt and in the process trying to offer a perspective.

Yet, tomorrow is another day and the Universe abounds.

Epilogue

I was between 6 and 7 years of age on this particular day. Zimbabwe is a landlocked country. It has distinct summer, winter, and rainy seasons, and of course spring. For the most part, the type of rainfall experienced there is convectional rainfall. Typically, the sun beats down on the earth at such a time or on such a day with the resultant evaporation taking place and leading to cloud formation and the onset of rain later on after that process. When the rain comes down, it really comes down. A torrent, a proper shower and you generally would rather be indoors or in shelter during that period. It was such a day on this day when I was in my father's car as he was running errands.

At that stage in my life in Zimbabwe, most of the farms were owned by white farmers and as was the case, the manual labour force would be black people. The relationship truly was master and servant. Due to the rugged terrain and the need for strong sturdy cars, particularly on the farms, most Zimbabweans and farmers, in particular, have pickup trucks which can either have or not have the canopy at the back. In this case, this particular lady, a white farmer I would assume had such a pickup truck but this one was without the canopy at the back. Which would then mean that, if someone was sitting at the back of this pickup truck, they would be exposed to the elements. Such was the case in this particular instance as in the back of this lady's pickup truck was a black man, a farm labourer I can safely assume.

Notably though, and most notably to me at the time, at the front of the car was the woman driving and in there with her, protected from the elements, was what would have been her pet dog. Hence, to bring it all together, as mentioned afore, on the day, the rain was pouring down torrentially and in the front of this car, was a white woman with her dog whilst the black man sat stuck, bare to the full measure of the elements. For a young mind, understanding such things is not the most natural ability and I wholly believe that it was on this day, to a large degree, that the function of social imbalance, politics, the human existential equation and question was singed into my mind and consciousness. Only equalled in later years by an all consuming desire to understand and address in some way such a presentation of existence.

At that stage of my development, the realisation then that I made was explainable mainly and only along racial lines. White people are bad, if not evil. With a clearer mindset and the maturity of years and further observation, I realised that the Irish for example were persecuted equally if not more by the English and by all accounts, both groups are wholly white. During the industrial revolution, British workers and their children faced horrendous working and living conditions, and they were white. In my own country tribal tension exists and existed such that post independence, a tribal civil war termed Gukurahundi could have erupted were it not for the intervention of a sensible political response on the part of some to the unrest. Both groups are and were wholly black. The first and second world wars which saw the innumerable deaths of many men were fought by nations which all housed white Europeans. The presence and proliferation of intra-racial conflict.

Hence, the function of race was not and is not the most explanatory. Consequently, in terms of social stratification, and social imbalance, a more substantive realisation became that of class. To at least begin to have a fairer society, the class struggle is the juggernaut we face. Karl Marx explained the idea of the conflict between classes and how it is intrinsic to human existence. Social stratification is an inescapable factor of human existence. If there is land, there will be landowners and those without, unless we all decide to give each human being a share of land. However, more notably, someone has to be in power and most notably, some will naturally have attributes which mean they end up "having more" than others, being more productive, skilled or intelligent which lands them superior to those around them. Social stratification, hierarchy, and class are seemingly inescapable social and existential phenomena. Absolute social equality is impossible if not dysfunctional. Role players are needed through every level of any social system. To abate this, however, it is fair to argue for equality under the law, equal human rights to all, accountability by all to these dictates and fair access to all the levers that allow each human individual to, if ultimately, self actualise along with the politics and philosophies to facilitate such an existence.

That said, the class struggle still does not do enough to explain and justify the presentation of human existence that shaped my mindset at that very nascent, tender, and vulnerable stage of my human existence. How can it ever be fair no matter how it is explained or validated that one human being should experience such a life in their lifetime? The humiliation, dehumanisation and emasculation to be passed on to his progeny. Where, who, and what is God to allow such an existence?

Equally so, what is life and how do we begin to justify who and what we are and what this life is under such a presentation of existence? To take it further we may speak of the general aspects of human suffering, malaise, banality, the function of just being; bullies, rapists, abusive partners, abusive parents, death, disease, illness, famine, pestilence, war, prejudice, lies, ignorance, opulence, deprivation, flora, fauna, and everything else beyond and in-between. Consequently, the realisation went from being the racial struggle and question, to being the class struggle and question to finally being the human struggle, the human existential struggle and question. How exponentially multifaceted, individual, and yet so collective it is, this life. Survival. The human condition. Who and what are we and what is this? That everlasting question. Ever more so if all can just stop and ask themselves if only for a moment, what am I doing with my life?! Perchance, something positive.

The irony however seems to me to be the irony of all ironies. It appears as though only in death do we or can we find out the true purpose of life. It seems certainly the most Dichotic of Dilemmas.

Consequently, suffice it to say…

"Nostalgia, some ancient memory long forgotten.
Hidden in the expansive annals of
experiences long past and forgotten.
What a bittersweet feeling.
A sweet and sorrowful yearning, for a time
that once was, but alas can never be.
A benevolent phantom, with a sweet scent that puts
one at ease and yet, yet just a bit perturbed.
A long lost friend. A forgotten smile.
A shared moment of supreme beauty with one
who is loved and close to the heart.
A peaceful secret waterfall.
The greenest and most abundant of forests. A beautiful,
radiant and picturesque sunset. Nostalgia.
It is a beautiful life.
Bitter sweet for it can never be otherwise. Else,
else we would never know the difference. The
Dichotic Dilemma, the fabric of life."

www.ingramcontent.com/pod-product-compliance
Lightning Source LLC
LaVergne TN
LVHW091554060526
838200LV00036B/833